THE ULTIMATE BOOK OF

Naughty GRAFFITI

THE WRITING ON THE WALL!

COMPILED AND EDITED BY

GREG KNIGHT

ROBSON BOOKS

First published in Great Britain in 2005 by Robson Books, The Chrysalis Building, Bramley Road, London W10 6SP.

An imprint of **Chrysalis** Books Group plc

Copyright © 2005 Greg Knight

British Library Cataloguing in Publication Data
A catalogue record for this title is available from the British Library.

ISBN 1 86105 895 0

Typeset by SX Composing DTP, Rayleigh, Essex
Printed by Creative Print & Design (Wales), Ebbw Vale

ON HOLIDAY LAST YEAR

EVENTS

VISITED SCOTLAND - WITNESSED 3 RARE SIGHTINGS

① GOLDEN EAGLE (HIGHLANDS) GLENCOE

② TWO MALE DEER (RUTTING) FIGHTING
        IN THE LOWLANDS

AND THE
MOST AMAZING   ③ A SCOTSMAN BYING A DRINK (SPENDING MONEY)
                        IN A ~~B~~ GLASGOW
SIGHT OF ALL   HIS OWN DRINK

                    CONTRIBUTED   TO

OFF COURSE SCOTLAND ~~GAVE THE WORLD~~ SOME IMPORTANT
        DISCOVERYS
~~Scotch Haggis~~ - WHISKEY - LOGIE BAIRD - EARLY TELEVISION
        TARMACADAM
AND OF COURSE THE INVENTION OFF A TIOLET SEAT (1874)

For

Major and Monty

MIND YOU
    THIS WAS LATER IMPROVED BY AN ENGLISHMAN
WHO THEN WAS LATER
    - ~~WHO~~ PUT A HOLE IN IT

AND COURSE SCOTLAND HAS HAD IT SHARE OF

NATIONAL ~~HEROES~~ ROB ROY -/ BONNIE PRINCE CHARLEY /
                                ROBBIE BURNS
~~ROBERT THE BRUCE~~ - AND NOT FORGETING BRAVEHEART

MEL GIBSON

                        SCOTTISH
    MY FATHER WAS ~~JEWISH~~ AND MY MOTHER
            JEW()
WAS . SCOTCH. SO THINGS HAVE ALWAYS BEEN ~~A~~ BIT
                SO I WAS CIRCUMS~~
TIGHT IN OUR FAMILY   'COS ALL JEWISH MEDITION WANT 25%
                                    OFF

GOOD EVENING LADIES AND ~~GENTLEMEN~~ ~~AND A~~
    AND ANYONE WHO IS NOT SURE WHICH THEY ARE

WHAT'S THE DERIVATION OF A SCOTTISH GENTLEMAN
                            CHR
A SCOTSMAN WHO PLAYS THE BAGPIPE

        BUT DOESN'T

CONTENTS

ACKNOWLEDGEMENTS

The author wishes to thank the following for their help, inspiration, advice, suggestions and assistance.

Ray Alan, Adrian Benson, Matthew Elliott, Timothy Kirkhope Esq. MEP, Luke Rainey, John M Taylor, Matthew Wennington and the late Arthur Worsley.

And a special thanks to all those anonymous scrawlers who regularly deface walls, posters, office noticeboards, university bulletin boards and urinals with their gems – and without whom this book would not have been possible.

Naughty Insulting, mischievous, discourteous, impolite, impish, wicked, coarse, vulgar.

Graffiti An inscription scratched or written on a surface, usually without the owner's consent. Messages or drawings, sometimes obscene, scribbled on notices or walls.

1. GIGGERET / CONDOM / 88 YR OLD / RAINING /
   CHEMIST / WHAT SIZE / AS LONG AS IT FIT,
   OVER A CAMEL

2. FATHER CUTTING THE GRASS WITH
   NO UNDERPANTS. WELL I HAD NO HAT ON
   MY BALD HEAD GOT SUNBURNT AND I GOT A
   STIFF NECK - SO ON WITH SAID LEMON
   MY UNDERPANTS OFF

3. DO YOU KNOW THE DIFFERENCE BETWEEN A CHICKEN
   BONE AND A PENIS - NO - WILL YOU COME TO
   A PICNIC WITH ME TOMORROW

4. I WEAR THE TROUSERS - YOU'LL NEVER GET
   INSIDE THESE KNICKERS . AND YOU WON'T
   IF YOU DON'T CHANGE YOUR ATTITUDE

5. I'M HAVING AN EVENING WITH HER DIET - I'VE BROKEN
   HER TOOTH

6. AIR PLANE / PILOT / AIR HOSTESS TRIM / DON'T
   RUSH HE GOT TO DO HIS CARGO CHECKS FIRST

7. ROSIN ARM - PETROL BOMB THROUGH THE WINDOW
   SOMEONE DROVE IN BEFORE IT REACHED THE FLOOR

INTRODUCTION

Anyone who has ever visited a public lavatory in the western world cannot have escaped noticing that one of the less than salubrious activities of certain members of the public is the dissemination of quips, jokes (usually smutty ones) and insults, by writing on the wall during the call of nature.

Inscribing messages on a wall for the benefit of others is certainly not a new phenomenon. It predates the punk era of the seventies, the flower power era of the sixties and even the Teddy Boy phase of the fifties. Indeed, it was our ancestors, the prehistoric cavemen, who were the originators of what is still today a thriving activity – graffiti.

The term *graffiti* is actually plural and the rarely used singular word is *graffito*. This term was first used by archaeologists to describe informal writings on ancient monuments and tombs. Today, any impertinent or impolite inscription on a wall is called graffiti, although the term is also used to describe images and artistic drawings. Now, as way back then, written items of graffiti cover a wide variety of subjects. However, most are satirical or insulting in tone and it is those that form the substance of this compilation.

The prevalence of graffiti writing grew vastly in popularity during the 1500s, with vulgar abuse and libel becoming rife. Back then, a surprisingly large number of instances concerned the female of the species – with women frequently making allegations relating to lack of propriety in other women, or other moral matters. Synonyms of the word *whore* were often scrawled on a female neighbour's wall, the most popular of these being *squirt*, *dirtyheels*, and *trull*.

One notorious graffito example of the times, which resulted in court proceedings being pursued, was:

Here lives Mrs Dungress who shows her arse in every alehouse
and who will pawn her muff for a drink.

Many people argue that those who commit acts of graffiti do so without taking responsibility for their actions because they hide behind anonymity. Unless the perpetrator is caught in the act, this is certainly true. Perhaps that is why the term today is generally used to describe *unauthorised* acts of property deface-ment involving paint and aerosol sprays. Of course, the perpe-trators in some instances are indeed vandals, causing criminal damage to the property of others – and it is certainly no part of the remit of this book to encourage or condone unlawful behaviour.

Although many of the most memorable doodles of wit and wisdom are inscribed without permission, in my view they are preferable to and certainly more enjoyable than the banal and childish so-called 'community drawings' commissioned by a number of UK local authorities and which are unfortunately seen painted on the walls of some of the buildings in our city centres.

Not all unauthorised graffiti is frowned upon and sometimes the graffiti artist is welcomed with open arms. In some licensed premises, for example, landlords have helpfully provided the necessary instruments to enable the art to flourish. Chalk and a blackboard, or a felt tip pen and a drawing board have been placed in the lavatory to actually encourage customers to have their say.

Neither are all graffiti artists uneducated yobs. A former Lord Chancellor, the late Lord Hailsham, a colourful and unpre-dictable figure, once indulged himself with the following piece of graffiti doggerel:

A Shakespearean actress played Puck,
In the course of which she got stuck
As she had never heard
Of that four-letter word
She said, 'Oh what rotten bad luck.'

In 2004, one such 'artist' spray-painted the formula for part of a chemical compound found in DNA on the road outside a lab where the double helix was unveiled fifty years ago. Atop the design the graffiti artist wrote the word *Phospholipase*. This led Professor Alan Dawson, Emeritus Professor of Biochemistry at the University of East Anglia in Norwich, to comment admiringly: 'It is a really nice bit of standard first- or second-year biochemistry.'

Perhaps predictably, the police and other academics in Cambridge took a different view and said they were trying to find the graffiti artist, who they acknowledged could be Britain's brightest vandal, so they could prosecute him. No doubt this was because councillors in the town had earlier launched a civic campaign to highlight the problem of graffiti and were operating a zero-tolerance approach.

The Keep Britain Tidy group has attacked pop stars and advertising groups for 'glamourising graffiti', claiming that unauthorised urban scrawl costs local councils across Britain some £27 million a year to remove. They say that graffiti makes streets 'squalid' and that 'people feel unsafe'. In support of this view they have criticised the street art display at Manchester's Urbis Museum and have blamed pop acts The Black-Eyed Peas and Christina Aguilera for featuring graffiti in their pop videos, making it appear 'edgy' and 'cool' to teenagers. 'Unauthorised graffiti has reached epidemic proportions,' they say.

Tony Blair would seem to agree with these views because in early 2004 his government introduced on-the-spot fines for those caught creating unauthorised graffiti. David Blunkett, then Home Secretary, went even further and just a few short months later announced that he was considering changing the law to give the police the power to arrest those dropping litter or scrawling graffiti.

However, not everyone is out to clobber the graffiti artist. His Royal Highness Prince Charles, no less, has recently become the champion of graffiti artists. In May 2004, the Prince's Trust supported the Urban Music Festival held at Earl's Court, which provided 'lessons in graffiti writing' to the 40,000 attendees. This support, as you might expect, was not without controversy, with one local councillor claiming that, 'Nobody, apart from the extreme practitioners of political correctness, dignifies graffiti with the name "art".'

For the purposes of this book, whether the activity is 'art' or not, whether in a particular case it is welcome and lawful, or illegal, irresponsible and arrestable, is, quite frankly, irrelevant. What matters here is: is it insulting, mischievous or discourteous – and is it amusing?

What is contained between these covers is certainly not as profound as the 'graffiti' handed down to Moses on tablets of stone. Indeed, some of the graffiti contained between these pages is rather nefarious, while other quips are comical. Some I find amusing, while a number of others I rather frown upon. However, in putting together this compilation my own taste is irrelevant, as to observe is not necessarily to approve.

However, I do think that what is contained between these covers does deserve to reach a wider audience, so ... read on.

GREG KNIGHT

SEPTEMBER 2005

1

IN THE GENTS

A selection of graffiti from the men's room:

If life is a waste of time, and time is a waste of life, then let's all get wasted together and have the time of our lives.

IF VOTING COULD REALLY CHANGE THINGS, IT WOULD BE ILLEGAL.

Two wrongs are only the beginning.

The problem with the gene pool is that there is no lifeguard.

A clear conscience is usually the sign of a bad memory.

Written on a mirror in a gents toilet in Leeds:

No wonder you always go home alone.

Fighting for peace is like screwing for virginity.

To do is to be. Descartes
To be is to do. Voltaire
Do be do be do. Frank Sinatra

Written in a washroom in the USA:

If pro is the opposite of con, then what is the opposite of progress? Congress!

God made cannabis. Man made beer.
Who do you trust?

Sign written above one of the urinals in a Northern public house:

Express Lane: Five beers or less.

And written above another:

To pee, or not to pee, that is the question.

And in another:

A HAPPY NEW YEAR TO ALL OUR READERS.

Scrawled high on the wall of another gents lavatory:

What are you looking up here for? ... Ashamed?

In a similar vein:

> If you can read this, you are not aiming in the right direction.

Seen in the lavatory of an inner city nightclub:

*Remember, it's not, 'How high are you?'
It's, 'Hi, how are you?'*

On the wall of a backstage lavatory at a Leicester working men's club:

It's hard to make a comeback when you haven't been anywhere.

BE CAREFUL, YOUR FAMILY'S FUTURE IS IN YOUR HANDS.

Probably the most common graffiti slogan in the UK during the 1950s and 1960s were the three words:

Kilroy was here.

In quite a few pub loos, someone – probably the pub landlord – would scribble an additional line underneath, so the verse became:

Kilroy was here ...
but only for the beer.

In one particular gents lavatory, the pub landlord used to frame copies of the current TV programme schedules for the benefit of his customers. When, one week, a programme was listed featuring the anti-porn campaigner Mary Whitehouse, someone defaced the Perspex casing with the words:

Kill Joy was here.

A sign on the wall above a gents urinal:

```
        NOTICE  TO  ALL  MEN

        We  aim  to  please.
        You  aim  too  please.

            The Management
```

PLAN TO BE SPONTANEOUS TOMORROW.

On the difference between men and women:

On the one hand, men will never
experience childbirth.
On the other hand, they can open all
their own jam jars.

Someone wrote in large white letters on the wall at an
American university:

JESUS SAVES!

And shortly afterwards, underneath some wag added in bright
red paint:

BUT WOULDN'T IT BE BETTER IF HE HAD INVESTED?

A statesman is a politician who didn't get caught.

In one loo, under the heading 'Heaven and Hell' someone
penned this diatribe:

**In heaven the English are the police, the French the
cooks, the Germans the mechanics, the Italians the
lovers, and the Swiss organise everything.
Now, in hell, the Germans are the police, the English
the cooks, the French the mechanics, the Swiss the
lovers, and the Italians organise everything.**

Love is an ocean of emotions, entirely surrounded by expenses.

GOING CAMPING IS LOITERING WITHIN TENT.

On a gents wall in a wine bar:

I feel sorry for all you teetotallers. Just think when you get up in the morning, that's the best you're gonna feel all day

At the time of Nixon's troubles over Watergate, graffiti seen on a lavatory wall in Washington was:

Where is Lee Harvey Oswald* now that his country needs him?

When my wife has one drink, she can't
feel it.
When she has two drinks, she can feel
it.
After her third drink, anybody can
feel it.

When the following line of graffiti appeared on a pub loo wall, it started off an avalanche of similar quips:

Two peanuts walk into a bar. One was a salted.

* President Kennedy's assassin.

Underneath which various folk then added:

I'm

And a dyslexic man walks into a bra.

A man walks into a bar with a slab of asphalt under his arm and says: 'A beer please, and one for the road.'

A car jump lead walks into a bar and the barman says, 'I'll serve you, but don't start anything.'

A sandwich walks into a bar and the barman says, 'Sorry, we don't serve food in here.'

A seal walks into a club ...

24 reasons why beer is better than women

1. You can enjoy a beer all month long.
2. Beer stains wash out.
3. You don't have to wine and dine beer.
4. Your beer will always wait patiently for you in the car while you play football.
5. When your beer goes flat, you toss it out.
6. Hangovers go away.
7. A beer label comes off without a fight.

8. Beer is never late.
9. Beer doesn't get jealous when you grab another beer.
10. When you go to a bar, you know you can always pick up a beer.
11. Beer never gets a headache.
12. After you've had a beer, the bottle is still worth five cents.
13. A beer won't get upset if you come home and have another beer.
14. If you pour a beer right, you'll always get good head.
15. A beer always goes down easy.
16. You can have more than one beer a night and not feel guilty.
17. You can share a beer with your friends.
18. You always know you're the first one to pop a beer.
19. Beer is always wet.
20. Beer doesn't demand equality.
21. You can have a beer in public.
22. A frigid beer is a good beer.
23. You don't have to wash a beer before it tastes good.
24. If you change beers you don't have to pay maintenance.

On women:

Don't trust anything that bleeds for five days
and doesn't die.

REMEMBER WHEN YOU GET HOME,
BEAUTY IS ONLY A LIGHT SWITCH AWAY.

The only thing she ever gives is in.

I looked up my wife's family tree. Most of her relatives are still climbing around in it.

She used to live in all the best hotels . . . one hour at a time.

My wife has an unlisted dress size.

All women scream the same way whether they're about to be devoured by a shark or if they feel a piece of seaweed touch their foot.

He's a gay called Heineken. He reaches the parts that other queers cannot reach.

IN 2004, THOUSANDS OF GERMANS TOOK TO THE STREETS TO PROTEST AT THE US INVASION OF IRAQ. THAT'S WHEN YOU KNOW YOU'VE ACCOMPLISHED SOMETHING - WHEN THE GERMANS THINK YOU'RE INVADING TOO MUCH.

Osama bin Laden - the final solution

Killing him will only create a martyr. Holding him prisoner will inspire his comrades to take hostages to demand his release. Therefore, I suggest we do neither. Let the SAS capture him, fly him to an undisclosed hospital and have surgeons quickly perform a complete sex change operation. Then we should return 'her' to Afghanistan to live as a woman under the Taliban.

Last year, the Irish SAS decided to help in the war against terrorism and bombed Battersea Dogs' Home . . .
They heard that 100 Afghans lived there!

My wife wasn't born yesterday – nobody could get that ugly in 24 hours.

Homosexuals are a pain in the bum.

I'd rather have a full bottle in front of me than a full frontal lobotomy.

My wife has no equals - only superiors.

If you want anything said, ask a woman.
If you want anything done, ask a man.

In one urinal, painters and decorators pinned up the following sign during decorations:

Shortly afterwards, the pub landlord was obliged to display a sign underneath, which read:

```
This is a warning,
not an instruction
```

Written on the mirror in a nightclub urinal:

Why don't you go home now? Your cage has been cleaned.

And:

YOU'VE GOT THE SORT OF FACE I'D LIKE TO SHAKE HANDS WITH.

You're the sort who gives idiots a bad name.

And:

It's not only the wall that's plastered – you're pissing on your shoe.

One public house in London displays a sign outside which reads:

Come inside – this is the place to play play table billiards.

On the gents lavatory door of the same pub, some wag has written:

Come inside – <u>this</u> is the place to play *pocket* billiards.

The Love Dress

A mother-in-law stops unexpectedly by the recently married couple's house. She rings the doorbell and steps into the house. She sees her daughter-in-law standing naked by the door. 'What are you doing?' she asks.

'I'm waiting for my husband to come home from work,' the daughter-in-law answers.

'But you're naked!' the mother-in-law exclaims.

'This is my love dress,' the daughter-in-law explains.

'Love dress? But you're naked!'

'My husband loves me to wear this dress! It makes him happy and it makes me happy. I would appreciate it if you would leave now because he will be home from work any minute.'

The mother-in-law leaves and on the way home she thinks about the love dress and decides to try it for herself. When she gets home she undresses, showers, puts on her best perfume and waits by the front door.

Finally her husband comes home. He walks in and sees her standing naked by the door. 'What are you doing?' he asks.

'This is my love dress,' she replies.

The husband replies: 'Well, it needs a bloody good ironing!'

> Atheism is a non-prophet
> organisation.

Before the Iraq war removed Saddam Hussein from power, the following was spotted scrawled in a US washroom:

I KNOW THE DIFFERENCE BETWEEN PRESIDENT GEORGE W BUSH AND SADDAM HUSSEIN . . .
ONE IS A DICTATOR WHO CAME TO POWER FOLLOWING A DUBIOUS ELECTION AND WHO REVELS IN IMPLEMENTING THE DEATH PENALTY. THE OTHER IS A GREASY IRAQI.

> I went to a bookstore and asked
> the saleswoman, 'Where's the
> self-help section?'
> She said if she told me, it
> would 'defeat the purpose'.

If you try to fail, and succeed, which have you done?

Some public houses try to stop the paint on the lavatory walls from being defaced by providing graffiti writing facilities. One landlord in the Midlands has recently provided a large gloss board and two felt-tip pens precisely for this purpose. The more banal comments are erased nightly but the humorous ones are allowed to remain, if not for posterity then at least for a month or two.

The provision of pens also allows smaller writing and hence longer contributions. Here are several such items, the first from a country pub:

A local farmer orders a high-tech milking machine. The equipment arrives when his wife is away, so he decides to test it on himself. He inserts his willie into the equipment, turns the switch on and ... everything else is automatic!!

He has a great time as the equipment provides him with as much pleasure as his wife does. When the fun is over, he finds that he cannot take the teat off. He reads the manual, but to no avail. He tries every button on the instrument, but still it continues. Panicking, he calls the supplier's Customer Service Hotline.

The farmer, by now totally exhausted, asks how he can remove the teat 'from the cow's udder'.

The Customer Service Manager tries to reassure him: 'Don't worry. The machine is programmed to release automatically after collecting about two litres of milk.'

Al Gore and the Clintons are flying on Air Force One. Bill looks at Al, chuckles, and says, 'You know, I could throw a one-hundred-dollar bill out the window right now and make one person very happy.'

Al shrugs his shoulders and says, 'Well, I would rather throw ten ten-dollar bills out the window and make ten people very happy.'

Hillary tosses her perfectly hair-sprayed hair and says, 'I could throw one hundred one-dollar bills out the window and make one hundred people happy.'

Bill and Hillary's daughter, Chelsea rolls her eyes, looks at all of them, and says, 'I could throw all three of you out the window and make two hundred and fifty million people happy.'

And:

A SMALL BOY ASKS HIS DAD, 'WHAT IS POLITICS?'
THE FATHER SAYS, 'WELL SON, LET ME TRY TO EXPLAIN IT THIS WAY. I'M THE BREADWINNER OF THE FAMILY, SO LET'S CALL ME CAPITALISM. YOUR MOM, SHE'S THE ADMINISTRATOR OF THE MONEY, SO WE'LL CALL HER THE GOVERNMENT. WE'RE HERE TO TAKE CARE OF YOUR NEEDS, SO

WE'LL CALL YOU THE PEOPLE. THE NANNY, WE'LL CONSIDER HER THE WORKING CLASS. AND YOUR BABY BROTHER, WE'LL CALL HIM THE FUTURE. NOW, THINK ABOUT THAT AND SEE IF THAT MAKES SENSE.'

SO THE LITTLE BOY GOES OFF TO BED THINKING ABOUT WHAT HIS DAD SAID. LATER THAT NIGHT, HE HEARS HIS BABY BROTHER CRYING SO HE GETS UP TO CHECK ON HIM. HE FINDS THAT THE BABY HAS SEVERELY SOILED HIS NAPPY. SO THE LITTLE BOY GOES TO HIS PARENTS' ROOM AND FINDS HIS MOTHER SOUND ASLEEP. NOT WANTING TO WAKE HER, HE GOES TO THE NANNY'S ROOM. FINDING THE DOOR LOCKED, HE PEEKS IN THE KEYHOLE AND SEES HIS FATHER IN BED WITH THE NANNY. HE GIVES UP AND GOES BACK TO BED.

THE NEXT MORNING THE LITTLE BOY SAYS TO HIS FATHER, 'DAD, I THINK I UNDERSTAND THE CONCEPT OF POLITICS NOW.' THE FATHER SAYS, 'GOOD, SON, TELL ME IN YOUR OWN WORDS WHAT YOU THINK POLITICS IS ALL ABOUT.'

THE LITTLE BOY REPLIES, 'WELL, WHILE CAPITALISM IS SCREWING THE WORKING CLASS, THE GOVERNMENT IS SOUND ASLEEP, THE PEOPLE ARE BEING IGNORED AND THE FUTURE IS IN DEEP SHIT.'

My mother never saw the irony in calling me a son-of-a-bitch.

Seen on a toilet wall in a nightclub:

I've been on so many blind dates, I should get a free dog.

Underneath which someone had scrawled:

And when I go on a blind date, I usually *get* the dog.

MY BROTHER HAS GONE TO THE PLACE OF ETERNAL REST . . . HE'S NOT DEAD – HE WORKS FOR THE POST OFFICE!

Message to all virgins
Thanks for nothing!

'I am' is reportedly the shortest sentence in the English language.
Well, believe me, 'I do' is certainly the longest sentence!

Unauthorised note pinned up outside a farmers' market, which had closed during the 2001 foot and mouth crisis:

<u>OFFICIAL NOTICE</u>
EVERYONE TO BE SLAUGHTERED

As a precautionary measure the Government has decided that in order to safeguard the future of British farming, everyone in the United Kingdom should be destroyed. This policy was agreed by the Prime Minister late last night at a secret policy meeting in Cumbria in front of five hundred angry farmers waving pitchforks, and the world's press. It was explained to the PM Tony Blair by his Agriculture Minister that, far from being their own fault, as simple country-dwelling folk, farmers could not be expected to deal with 'citified new-fangled nonsense' such as 'insurance' and 'vaccinations'. Mr Blair concluded that the only surefire way of protecting farmers is to ensure that all living things within a hundred-mile radius of the British coastline are immediately exterminated.

The army and police have been called in, and the slaughter of men, women and children is due to begin at midnight. It is expected that within days, mass burning of villages will commence, with all people in Manchester due for destruction a week on Tuesday. Television companies are reported to be overjoyed at this news. Channel 4 is already planning a themed game show, *Big Barbecue* where the public will ring in and vote on which part of the country is to be incinerated first; and ITV will be showing 24-hour coverage.

Farming expert Dr Jeremy Scumamore (Labour peerage pending) commented that these measures were 'a proportionate and measured response to the crisis - the Government's proposal is entirely understandable. I fully support them,' he said as he booked his flight to New York.

It is expected that within two weeks of this policy being carried out foot and mouth disease will be entirely eradicated from the United Kingdom.

The Prime Minister's Press Secretary said that the plan was 'unlikely to affect the date of the next General Election'.

✳ *IMPOTENCE IS NATURE'S WAY OF SAYING, 'NO HARD FEELINGS'.*

My girlfriend always laughs during sex – no matter what she's reading.

I have been married twice and both my wives were marvellous housekeepers. When we split, they kept the house.

Seen on a nightclub lavatory wall:

I let my girlfriend down to be here tonight . . .
Don't worry. I'll blow her up again when I get home.

Seen on the wall in a US washroom:

A guy gets home late one night and his wife says, 'Where the hell have you been?'

'I was out getting a tattoo.'

'A tattoo? What kind of tattoo did you get?'

'I got a hundred-dollar bill tattooed on my penis.'

'What the hell were you thinking? Why did you get a hundred-dollar bill tattooed on your penis?'

'Well, number one, I like to watch my money grow ... Number two, once in a while, I like to play with my money ... And lastly, instead of you going out shopping, you can stay right here at home and blow a hundred bucks anytime you want!'

104 reasons why it's better to be a man

1. Phone conversations last thirty seconds.
2. Queues for the loo are eighty per cent shorter.
3. You don't have to lug a bag of 'necessary' items with you everywhere you go.
4. You get extra thanks for the slightest act of thoughtfulness.
5. You never have to clean the toilet.
6. Wedding plans take care of themselves.
7. Chocolate is just another snack.
8. Flowers or Sellotape can fix everything.
9. You never have to worry about anyone else's feelings.
10. Same work – more pay.

11. If you don't call your friend when you say you will, he won't tell everyone that you've changed.
12. New shoes don't cut, blister, or mangle your feet.
13. You can drive a car ...
14. Even in a crowded car park.
15. You don't need a second opinion to know if your bum looks big in whatever you're wearing.
16. You can buy the first thing you see without having to come back three hours later.
17. *Match of the Day*.
18. You don't have to monitor your friends' sex lives.
19. You can open all your own jars.
20. Old friends don't give you a hard time if you've lost or gained weight.
21. Dry cleaners and hairdressers don't rob you blind.
22. When channel surfing, you don't have to stop on every shot of someone crying.
23. Your bum and your chest are never factors in job interviews.
24. All your orgasms are real.
25. A beer gut does not make you invisible to the opposite sex.
26. Movie nudity is virtually always female.
27. People expect you to masturbate.
28. You can go to the toilet without a support group.
29. Your last name stays put.
30. You can leave a hotel bed unmade.
31. When your work is criticised, you don't panic that everyone secretly hates you.
32. You can kill your own food.
33. The garage is yours, all yours.

34. *Baywatch.*
35. Nobody secretly wonders if you swallow.
36. You can't get pregnant.
37. You can belch with impunity.
38. You can be showered and ready in ten minutes.
39. Sex means never having to worry about your reputation.
40. You can get to places on time.
41. If someone forgets to invite you to something, he or she can still be your friend.
42. Timetables and fax machines don't confuse you.
43. You understand why *Beavis and Butthead* is funny.
44. None of your co-workers have the power to make you cry.
45. You don't have to shave below your neck.
46. People aren't talking about you all the time.
47. If you're thirty-four and single, nobody gives a toss.
48. You can write your name in the snow.
49. You don't have to bother having a proper conversation with your friends down at the pub.
50. Everything on your face stays its original colour.
51. You can get through a day off work without daytime television.
52. The offside rule is not a mystery to you.
53. You can quietly enjoy a car ride from the passenger seat.
54. You get to think about sex ninety per cent of your waking hours (and one hundred per cent of your sleeping hours).
55. You can wear a white shirt in the rain.
56. Three pairs of shoes are more than enough for most of your life.
57. You can boast about the number of people you've slept with.

58. You can say anything and not worry about what people think.
59. Foreplay is optional.
60. Michael Bolton and Barry Manilow don't live in your universe.
61. Nobody stops telling a good dirty joke when you walk in the room.
62. You can whip your shirt off on a hot day.
63. You don't have to clean your flat if the meter reader is coming by.
64. You never feel compelled to stop a pal from getting laid.
65. Car mechanics tell you the truth.
66. You don't give a toss if no one notices your new haircut.
67. You can watch a game in silence with your mate for hours without even thinking, *he must be mad at me.*
68. The world is your urinal.
69. You never misconstrue innocuous statements to mean your lover is about to leave you.
70. You can play and enjoy computer games.
71. Hot wax never comes near your legs.
72. One mood, all the time.
73. You can admire Julia Roberts without starving yourself to look like her.
74. You can remember the punch lines to jokes.
75. You know at least twenty ways to open a beer bottle.
76. You can sit with your knees apart no matter what you are wearing.
77. Grey hair and wrinkles add character.
78. You never have to leave the room to make an emergency knicker adjustment.

79. A wedding dress costs over £1000, but morning suit hire is only £45.
80. You can vomit without being accused of bulimia.
81. With 400 million sperm per shot, you could double the Earth's population in fifteen tries – at least in theory – and trying would be fun.
82. You don't take a taste of others' desserts.
84. If you retain water, it's in a glass.
85. The remote is yours and yours alone.
86. People never glance at your chest when you're talking to them.
87. You can sit in a pub on your own without some old codger trying to chat you up.
88. You can drop by to see a friend without bringing a little gift.
89. Stag nights are much more fun than hen nights.
90. You have a normal and healthy relationship with your mother.
91. You can buy condoms without the shopkeeper imagining you naked.
92. You needn't pretend you're 'freshening up' when you go for a shit.
93. Someday you'll be a dirty old man.
94. You can rationalise any behaviour with the handy phrase, 'F**k it!'
95. If another bloke shows up at the party in the same outfit, you might become best mates.
96. You can teach your friends' children swear words.
97. You never have to miss a sexual opportunity because you're not in the mood.

98. If something mechanical doesn't work, you can bash it with a hammer and throw it across the room.
99. A week's holiday requires only one suitcase.
100. Porn movies are designed with your mind in mind.
101. You can run without looking like two boys fighting inside a large sack.
102. Your pals can be trusted never to trap you with: 'So . . . notice anything different?'
103. You can play football instead of going to a family party – and not feel guilty.
104. Throwing and catching objects is possible.

BIGAMY IS HAVING ONE WIFE TOO MANY. MONOGAMY IS THE SAME.

Women might be able to fake orgasms but men can fake whole relationships.

My parents saw the president they loved get shot in the head.
I just saw my president *get* head.

Clinton lied. A man might forget where he parks or where he lives but he never forgets oral sex no matter how bad it is.

Did you hear about the Irishman who got kicked out of *Riverdance* for using his arms?

Support bacteria. They're the only culture some people have.

YOU'RE NOT REALLY DRUNK IF YOU CAN LIE ON THE FLOOR WITHOUT HANGING ON.

The World Wide Web brings people together because no matter what kind of a twisted sexual mutant you happen to be, you've got millions of friends out there. Type in to your search: 'Find people that have sex with goats that are on fire' and the computer will say, 'Specify type of goat.'

A little philosophy:

Never read the fine print. There ain't no way you're going to like it.

If you let a smile be your umbrella, then your arse will get soaking wet.

The only two things we do with greater frequency in middle age are urinate and attend funerals.

The trouble with bucket seats is that not everybody has the same size bucket.

To err is human, to forgive – highly unlikely.

There are only two reasons to sit in the back row of an aeroplane . . .
Either you have diarrhoea or you're anxious to meet people who do.

- No. There are three reasons. It's safer to sit at the back, cos I have yet to hear of an aeroplane backing into a mountain!

I phoned the Incontinence Hotline and the bastards said, 'Can you hold, please?'

Statistics show that seventy-seven per cent of all the mentally ill live in poverty . . .
I'm intrigued by the twenty-three per cent who are apparently doing quite well for themselves.

Honesty is the key to a relationship. If you can fake that, you're in.

DO YOU KNOW THE WATFORD TURN OFF?
YES - I MARRIED HER.

Man is incomplete until he is married. Then he is finished.

My girlfriend told me I should be more affectionate. So I got myself two girlfriends.

My wife dresses to kill. She also cooks the same way.

A bartender is just a pharmacist with a limited inventory.

A note pinned on the gents lavatory wall in a bar which specialises in entertainment:

A guy walks into a bar with a pet alligator by his side. He puts the alligator up on the bar. He turns to the astonished patrons. 'I'll make you a deal. I'll open this alligator's mouth and place my genitals inside. Then the alligator will close his mouth for one minute. He'll then open his mouth

and I'll remove my penis unscratched. In return for witnessing this spectacle, each of you will buy me a drink.'

The crowd murmur their approval. The man stands up on the bar, drops his pants, and places his privates in the alligator's open mouth. The alligator closes his mouth as the crowd gasp.

After a minute, the man grabs a beer bottle and raps the alligator hard on the top of its head, its jaws open and he is released unharmed. The crowd cheer and the first of his free drinks is duly delivered.

The man stands up again and makes another offer. 'I'll pay anyone £100 who's also willing to give it a try.' A hush falls over the crowd.

After a while, a hand goes up in the back of the bar. A blonde woman timidly speaks up. 'I'll try,' she says, 'provided you promise not to hit me on the head with the beer bottle.'

I have Anal Glaucoma – I just can't see my arse coming to work today.

Seen in the gents at a motorway café:

Have you ever noticed ... Anybody going slower than you is an idiot, and anyone going faster than you is a maniac?

NEVER HAS A TRUER WORD BEEN SPOKEN ...

Smart man + smart woman = romance

Dumb man + dumb woman = pregnancy

Smart man + dumb woman = affair

Dumb man + smart woman = marriage
Smart boss + smart employee = profits
Smart boss + dumb employee = production
Dumb boss + smart employee = promotion
Dumb boss + dumb employee = overtime

Man will pay $2.00 for a $1.00 item he needs.

Woman will pay $1.00 for a $2.00 item that she doesn't need.

Woman worries about the future until she gets a husband.

Man never worries about the future until he gets a wife.

Successful man makes more money than his wife can spend.

Successful woman is one who finds such a man.

To be happy with a man, you must love him a little and understand him a lot.

To be happy with a woman, you must love her a lot and not try to understand her at all.

Men wake up as good-looking as they went to bed.

Women somehow deteriorate overnight.

Woman marries a man expecting he will change ... he doesn't.

Man marries a woman expecting she won't change ... she does.

Married men live longer than single men; however, they are also more willing to die.

Married men should forget about their mistakes. No

point in two people remembering the same thing. Woman has the last word in any argument. Anything a man says after that is the beginning of a new argument.

✳ MY WIFE HAS THE BODY OF A GOD - BUDDHA!

The Japanese government have sent 500 tons of Viagra to the USA after hearing that they were having trouble with their elections.

A shopkeeper moves to a new and better venue, and many friends send flowers for his Grand Opening. It becomes clear that someone at a florist's shop has made a significant mistake when one of the huge bouquets arrives and the owner reads the card: it says, 'Rest in Peace.'

Somewhat upset, he calls the number on the enclosed florist's card and asks what was going on. It is clear from his voice that he is really incensed. But he calms down somewhat after the florist responds to him, saying, 'Sir, I do apologise for this mistake. However, instead of being so angry yourself, why don't you consider the other side? Somewhere today there is a funeral taking place, and on one of the bouquets, the card reads, "Congratulations on your new location."'

THE BIGGEST CHINESE TAKEAWAY IN THE WORLD IS IN BIRMINGHAM - IT'S CALLED MG ROVER.

Alzheimer's advantage: New friends every day.

Marry your mistress and create a job vacancy.

*Seen written in the dirt on the back of a van:
Driver carries no cash – he's married.*

Now that food has replaced sex in my life, I can't even get into my *own* pants.

The only thing a Polish woman gets on her wedding night that is guaranteed to be long and hard is a new surname.

There are two theories about arguing with women.
Neither one works.

A GOOD WIFE ALWAYS FORGIVES HER HUSBAND WHEN SHE'S WRONG.

My wife keeps complaining that I never listen to her – or something like that!

You never really learn to swear until you learn to drive.

FIGHT CRIME – SHOOT BACK

Paddy and Paddy go out one day and each buy a pig. When they get home, Paddy turns to Paddy and says, 'Paddy, me ol' mate, how we gonna tell who owns which ruddy pig?'

Paddy says: 'Well Paddy, I'll cut one a ta ears off my ruddy pig, and ten we can tell 'em apart.'

'Ah tat'd be grand,' says Paddy.

This works fine until a couple of weeks later when Paddy storms into the house. 'Paddy,' he says. 'Your ruddy pig has chewed the ear off my ruddy pig. Now we got two ruddy pigs with one ear each. How we gonna tell who owns which ruddy pig?'

'Well Paddy,' says Paddy. 'I'll cut ta other ear off my ruddy 'pig, ten we'll 'ave two ruddy pigs and only one of them will 'ave an ear.'

'Ah tat'd be grand,' says Paddy.

Again this works fine until a couple of weeks later when

Paddy again storms into the house. 'Paddy,' he says. 'Your ruddy pig has chewed the other ear offa my ruddy pig. Now we got two ruddy pigs with no ruddy ears. How we gonna tell who owns which ruddy pig?'

'Ah tis is serious, Paddy,' says Paddy. 'I'll tell ya what I'll do. I'll cut ta tail offa my ruddy pig. Ten we'll av two ruddy pigs with no ruddy ears and only one ruddy tail.'

'Ah tat'd be grand,' says Paddy.

Another couple of weeks go by, and you guessed it, Paddy storms into the house once more. 'PADDY!' shouts Paddy. 'YOUR RUDDY PIG HAS CHEWED THE RUDDY TAIL OFFA MY RUDDY PIG AND NOW WE GOT TWO RUDDY PIGS WITH NO RUDDY EARS AND NO RUDDY TAILS! HOW THE HELL ARE WE GONNA RUDDY WELL TELL 'EM APART!!!!!!!!!!!!!!?'

'Ah stuff it,' says Paddy. 'How's about you have the black one, and I'll have the white one?'

And a fairytale:

Once upon a time, in a land far away, a beautiful, independent, self assured princess happened upon a frog as she sat contemplating ecological issues on the shores of an unpolluted pond in a verdant meadow near her castle.

The frog hopped into the Princess's lap and said: 'Elegant lady, I was once a handsome prince, until an evil witch cast a spell upon me. One kiss from you, however, and I will turn back into the dapper, young prince that I am and then, my sweet, we can marry and set up housekeeping in yon castle where you can prepare my meals, clean my clothes, bear my children, and forever feel grateful and happy doing so.'

That night, on a repast of lightly sauteed frogs' legs seasoned in a white wine and onion cream sauce, she chuckled to herself and thought, I don't bloody think so.

The following non-PC note was pinned up by the side of a TV set in a public bar:

Three Chinese men die and go to heaven. God meets them at the Pearly Gates. He tells them that they can only come in if they have led a good life. He asks the first one if he thinks he deserves to come in.

He says, 'I think so.'

'Well I will set you a task,' says God, and he asks him to lift a large rock above his head, which he does easily. 'OK, you can come in.'

He asks the next man the same question and sets the same task, which he does with ease. 'OK, you can come in too.'

He sets the exact same task for the third man. The third Chinese man goes over to the rock and cannot lift it. He tries again and again, struggling. God turns to him and says … 'You are the weakest Chink, goodbye.'

Free Beer!!!

A new guy in town walks into a bar and reads a sign that hangs over the bar: FREE BEER! FREE BEER FOR THE PERSON WHO CAN PASS THE TEST!

So the man asks the bartender what the test is.

Bartender: 'Well, first you have to drink that whole gallon of pepper tequila, the WHOLE thing at once – and you can't make a face while doing it. Second, there's an alligator out back with a sore tooth – you have to remove it with your bare hands. Third, there's a woman upstairs who's never had an orgasm – you gotta make things right for her.'

Man: 'Well, as much as I would love free beer, I won't do it. You have to be nuts to drink a gallon of pepper tequila and then get crazier from there.'

As time goes on and the man drinks a few, he asks, 'Wherez zat teeqeelah?' He grabs the gallon of tequila with both hands and downs it with a big slurp and tears streaming down his face. Next, he staggers out back and soon all the people inside hear the most frightening roaring and thumping, then silence. The man staggers back into the bar, his shirt ripped and big scratches all over his body. 'Now,' he says. 'Where's that woman with the sore tooth?'

A man takes the day off work and decides to go out golfing. He is on the second hole when he notices a frog sitting next to the green. He thinks nothing of it and is about to swing when he hears, 'Ribbit 9-Iron.'

The man looks around and doesn't see anyone. Again he hears, 'Ribbit 9-Iron.' He looks at the frog and decides to prove the frog wrong, puts the club away, and grabs a 9-Iron. – Boom! He hits it ten inches from the cup. He is shocked by this. He says to the frog, 'Wow that's amazing. You must be a lucky frog, eh?'

The frog replies, 'Ribbit Lucky frog.'

The man decides to take the frog with

him to the next hole. 'What do you think, frog?' the man asks.

'Ribbit 3-Wood.'

The man takes out a 3-Wood and – Boom! Hole in one.

The man is befuddled and doesn't know what to say. By the end of the day, the man has played the best game of golf in his life and he asks the frog, 'OK, where to next?'

The frog replies, 'Ribbit Las Vegas.'

They go to Las Vegas and the man says, 'OK frog, now what?'

The frog says, 'Ribbit Roulette.'

Upon approaching the roulette table, the man asks, 'What do you think I should bet?' The frog replies, 'Ribbit three thousand dollars, black 6.'

Now, this is a million-to-one shot to win, but after the golf game the man figures what the heck – Boom! Tons of cash comes sliding back across the table.

The man takes his winnings and buys the best room in the hotel. He sits the frog down and says, 'Frog, I don't know how to repay you. You've won me all this money and I am forever grateful.'

The frog replies, 'Ribbit kiss me.'

The man figures why not, since after all the frog did for him, he deserves it.

With a kiss, the frog turns into a gorgeous fifteen-year-old girl …

'And that, your honour, is how the girl ended up in my room. So help me God, or my name is not William Jefferson Clinton.'

Assassins do it from behind.

Sam arrives in his office one morning to find his colleague roaring with laughter. 'What's so funny?' he asks.

His mate says, 'I made a hilarious Freudian slip this morning.'

'What's a Freudian slip?' Sam asks.

'It's when you mean to say something, but what comes out is what's really on your mind. This morning, I was queuing at the station to buy my ticket to Tooting, and noticed the girl behind the counter had huge breasts. When I eventually got to the front of the queue, I asked for a ticket to Titting. She went bright red and the whole queue were in fits.'

The next morning, Sam is laughing when his mate arrives at work. 'What's the matter?' his mate asks.

'I had one of your Freudian slips this morning. I was sitting in the kitchen this morning having breakfast, when instead of saying to my wife, "Pass the milk please, dear," I say, "Piss off you ugly cow, you've ruined my life."'

More questions and answers:

What do you call a smart blonde?
A golden retriever.

How do you know when you're leading a sad life?
When a nymphomaniac tells you, 'Let's just be
friends.'

WHY DON'T BUNNIES MAKE NOISE WHEN THEY HAVE SEX?
BECAUSE THEY HAVE COTTON BALLS.

WHAT HAS A BUNCH OF LITTLE BALLS
AND SCREWS OLD LADIES?
A BINGO MACHINE.

What's the difference between a porcupine and a
Ford Ka?
A porcupine has the pricks on the outside.

Why did God create alcohol?
So ugly old crows could have sex too.

What did the blonde bimbo say when she
found out she was pregnant?
'Are you sure it's mine?'

If you are having sex with two women and one more walks in, what do you have?
Divorce proceedings!

Why is being in the Military like having sex?
The closer you get to discharge, the better you feel..

What does a 75-year-old woman have between her breasts?
Her navel.

Did you hear about the dyslexic Rabbi?
He walks around saying, 'Yo.'

What do you call an Irish farmer with a sheep under each arm?
A pimp.

How do you get a sweet little 80-year-old lady to say, 'F**k'?
Get another sweet little 80-year-old lady to yell, 'Bingo!'

What do you call it when an Italian has one
arm shorter than the other?
A speech impediment.

What does it mean when the flag at the Bank
is flying at half mast?
They're hiring.

WHEN I WAS YOUNG I HAD FUN KNOCKING
ON DOORS AND RUNNING AWAY ...
I STILL DO IT - BUT NOW I WORK FOR
PARCELFORCE

Here's to the best time of my life,
spent in the arms of another
man's wife ...
Here's to my mother!

HOME IS WHERE YOU CAN SAY ANYTHING
YOU LIKE, COS NOBODY LISTENS TO YOU
ANYWAY.

I live in my own little world, but it's OK, they know me here.

When you stop believing in Santa Claus is
when you start getting clothes for Christmas!

41

Seen in the loo at a railway station:

The only way to be sure of catching a train in Britain today is to miss the one before.

I DON'T HAVE A BIG EGO, I'M WAY TOO COOL FOR THAT.

Real happiness is when you marry a girl for love – and find out that she has money.

I had a sweater at Christmas … Typical. I really wanted a screamer or a moaner.

Written on the wall of a French bar:

Men: no shirt on – no service
Women: no shirt on – NO CHARGE!

I saw a woman wearing a sweatshirt with 'Guess' on it. I said, 'Thyroid problem?'

I see your IQ test results were negative.

I don't approve of political jokes. I've seen too many of them get elected.

THERE ARE TWO SIDES TO EVERY DIVORCE: YOURS AND RATBAG'S.

Hell hath no fury like a woman's corns.

WANTED

MEANINGFUL OVERNIGHT RELATIONSHIP.

Travel is very educational. I can now say 'Diarrhoea' in seven different languages.

After all is said and done, usually more is said than done.

I am a nobody. Nobody is perfect. Therefore I am perfect.

I will never be unfaithful to my wife – I love the house too much

How can you tell if your wife is dead?
The sex doesn't change, but the dishes pile up.

No one ever says, 'It's only a game' when their team is winning.

How come we choose from just two people for president and fifty for Miss America?

I need someone really bad ... Are you really bad?

How long a minute is depends on what side of the bathroom door you're on.

BEAUTY IS IN THE EYE OF THE BEER HOLDER.

Middle age is when you choose your cereal for the fibre, not the toy.

Every time I walk into a singles bar I can hear my mother's wise words: 'Don't pick that up, you don't know where it's been.'

Why is it when a man talks dirty to a woman it's sexual harassment, but when a woman talks nasty to a man it's £1 a minute?

A mortician is working late one night. It is his job to examine the dead bodies before they are sent off to be buried or cremated. As he examines the body of Mr Spooner, who is about to be cremated, he makes an amazing discovery: Spooner has the longest penis he has ever seen!

'I'm sorry, Mr. Spooner,' the mortician mutters, 'but I can't send you off to be cremated with a tremendously huge penis like this. It has to be saved for posterity.' And the mortician uses his tools to remove the dead man's willie.

The mortician stuffs his prize into a briefcase and takes it home. The first person he shows is his wife. 'I have something to show you that you won't believe,' he says, and he opens his briefcase.

'Oh, my God!' she screams. 'Spooner is dead.'

Why does it take hundreds of millions of sperm to fertilise one egg?
Because they never stop to ask for directions.

A redneck, a sheep, and a dog are survivors of a terrible shipwreck. They find themselves stranded on a desert island. After being there a while, they get into the habit of going to the beach every evening to watch the sun go down. One particular evening, the sky is red with beautiful cirrus clouds, the breeze is warm and gentle; a perfect night for romance. As they sit there, the sheep starts looking better and better to the redneck.

Soon, he leans over to the sheep and puts his arm around it. But the dog gets jealous, growling fiercely until the redneck takes his arm from around the sheep. After that, the three of them continue to enjoy the sunsets together, but there is no more cuddling.

A few weeks pass by, and lo and behold, there is another shipwreck. The only survivor is a beautiful young woman, the most beautiful woman the redneck has ever seen. She is in a pretty bad way when they rescue her, but he slowly nurses her back to health. When the young maiden is well enough, he introduces her to their evening beach ritual.

It is another beautiful evening: red sky, cirrus clouds, a warm and gentle breeze; perfect for a night of romance. Pretty soon, the redneck starts to get 'those feelings' again. He fights them as long as he can, but he finally gives in and leans over to the young woman, cautiously, and whispers in her ear … 'Would you mind taking the dog for a walk?'

A PROTESTANT IN NORTHERN IRELAND DIDN'T WANT HIS WIFE MISTAKEN FOR A CATHOLIC IN THE LOYALIST AREA WHERE THEY LIVED – SO HE WROTE 'PROTESTANT' ON THE BACK OF HER BLOUSE ... SHE CAME BACK WITH OVER £1000 COS HE COULDN'T SPELL PROPERLY.

THE TEETH IN MY WIFE'S MOUTH ARE ALL EVEN – IT'S THE ODD ONES THAT ARE BLOODY MISSING!

And underneath someone added:

So what. My wife has more fillings than Spud-U-Like.

21 reasons why guitars are better than women

1. A guitar has a volume knob.
2. If you break a guitar's G-string, it only costs £1 for a new one.
3. You can make a guitar scream as loud as you want it to.
4. You can unplug a guitar.
5. You can finger a guitar for hours without it complaining it wants more.

6. Other people can play your guitar without it getting upset.

7. You can finger a guitar in public and get applause, not arrested.

8. You can have a guitar any colour you want and no one will care.

9. You can make your guitar as tight as you want it just by turning a peg.

10. If your guitar doesn't make sounds you like, you can retune it.

11. You can use four fingers at a time on a guitar.

12. If your guitar strings are too heavy, you can just get a lighter set.

13. You can have a guitar professionally adjusted to your liking.

14. If you scratch a guitar's back, it's unintentional, not a requirement.

15. You can go to a guitar shop and play all the guitars you want for free.

16. It's good to have a guitar that's stretched out.

17. You can take lessons on how to play a guitar without feeling embarrassed.

18. You can rent a guitar without worrying about who rented it before you.

19. You can play the guitar with your bare fingers and no protective covering.

20. You can get rich playing a guitar, not broke.

21. A guitar doesn't take half of everything you own when you sell it.

Necrophilia: that uncontrollable urge to crack open a cold one.

JOIN THE ARMY, MEET INTERESTING PEOPLE, AND KILL THEM.

And, finally in this section, the following was observed written atop a wall full of graffiti in a London pub lavatory:

Next year this wall comes out in paperback.

2

IN THE LADIES

On men:

The best way to a man's heart is to saw his breastplate open.

No matter how good he looks, some other girl is sick and tired of putting up with his crap.

I still miss my ex - but my aim is improving.

Show me a man with both feet firmly on the ground, and I'll show you a man who can't get his pants off.

I think men who have a pierced ear are better prepared for marriage.
They've experienced pain - and have bought jewellery.

If swimming is so good for your figure, how do you explain whales?

I have a nice body. It's in my trunk.

I JUST LET MY MIND WANDER, AND IT DIDN'T COME BACK.

Make it idiot-proof and someone will make a better idiot.

Politicians and nappies need to be changed ... often for the same reason.

20 reasons why women are better than guitars

1. Women are more fun when the power goes off.
2. You can't get your guitar wet.
3. Have you ever tried to screw a guitar?
4. The input to a guitar is only $\frac{1}{4}$ inch.
5. A guitar won't beg to be played.

6. It's no fun to tie your guitar to a bed and spray whipped cream on it.
7. When playing a guitar, you can use your teeth, but not your tongue.
8. Guitars aren't aggressive.
9. A guitar won't return your favours.
10. You need two hands to make a guitar scream.
11. A guitar won't scratch *your* back.
12. A guitar won't drive you home if you're too drunk.
13. A guitar doesn't care who plays it.
14. You can't play two guitars at once.
15. You can't fall in love with a guitar (well, perhaps you can, but they can't love you back).
16. It's a lot more fun to stretch out a woman than guitar strings.
17. Guitar lessons aren't free and aren't as much fun.
18. If you want a couple of little guitars, you'll have to buy them.
19. You can't marry a rich guitar.
20. Even a good guitar won't usually last a whole lifetime.

Make love, not war ...
Oh Hell, do both, get married!

On diets:

The second day of a diet is always easier
than the first.
By the second day you're off it.

Here's a great diet. You're allowed to eat anything you
want, but you must eat it with naked fat people.

The first thing you'll lose on a diet
is your sense of humour.

I suppose that Scotsmen wear kilts because it's easier
to run with your kilt up than your pants down!

**A woman's rule of thumb: If it has tyres or
testicles, you're going to have trouble with it.**

**DON'T WORRY GIRLS.
LIFE'S NOT THAT BAD.
YOUR PARENTS RUIN THE FIRST HALF AND
YOUR CHILDREN THE REST.**

At the bottom of a wall which contained a wide variety of graffiti – some insulting, some philosophical, some sad, but all of it interesting – someone wrote:

Isaac Newton was wrong ...
there are no laws of graffiti.

How do you know when you're really ugly?
Dogs hump your leg with their eyes closed.

Middle age is when your knees buckle and your belt won't.

A BiS
I never travel on the tube
- I suffer from Riffraffobia.

I'VE DECIDED THAT TO RAISE MY GRADES I MUST LOWER MY STANDARDS.

Work like you don't need the money.
Love like you've never been hurt.
And
Dance like you do when nobody's watching.

Sometimes I wake up grumpy; other times I let him sleep.

Professionals

Three men and a woman were sitting at the bar talking about their professions.
The first man says, 'I'm a YUPPIE ... you know ... Young, Urban, Professional.'
The second guy says, 'I'm a DINK ... you know ... Double Income, No Kids.'
The third man says, 'I'm a RUB ... you know ... Rich, Urban, Biker.'
They turn to the woman and ask her, 'What are you?'
She replies, 'I'm a W I F E ... you know ... Wash, Iron, F**k, Etc.'

Inside me, there's a thin woman crying to get out - but I can usually shut the bitch up with biscuits.

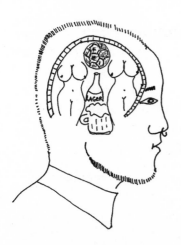

Brain of a typical male   *Brain of a typical female*

Behind every successful man is a surprised woman.

Women's one-liners:

I'm not your type. I'm not inflatable.
An erection does not count as personal growth.
This isn't an office. It's Hell with fluorescent lighting.
I pretend to work. They pretend to pay me.
If I throw a stick, will you leave?
If I want to hear the patter of little feet, I'll put shoes on my cat.
Did the aliens forget to remove your anal probe?
See no evil, hear no evil, and date no evil.
Sarcasm is just one more service we offer.

Whatever kind of look you were going for, you missed.

I am doing my best to imagine you with a personality.

Okay, okay, I take it back. Un-F**k you!

Not all men are annoying. Some are dead.

Too many freaks, not enough circuses.

And which dwarf are you?

How do I set a laser printer to stun?

It's not the size that counts, it's the ... umm ... actually, it is the size.

A man leaves work one Friday afternoon. But, it being payday, instead of going home, he stays out the entire weekend partying with the boys and spending his entire week's wages.

When he finally appears at home on Sunday night he is confronted by a very angry wife and is barraged for nearly two hours with a tirade befitting his actions. Finally his wife stops the nagging and simply says to him, 'How would you like it if you didn't see me for two or three days?'

To which he replies, 'That would be fine with me.'

Monday goes by and he doesn't see his wife. Tuesday and Wednesday come and go with the same results. Come Thursday, the swelling goes down just enough, where he can see her a little out of the corner of his left eye.

When women are depressed they either eat or go shopping ...
Men invade another country.

Why does chocolate make my clothes shrink?

Do you realise that in forty years' time, we'll have thousands of old ladies waddling around with tattoos on their backsides?

Money can't buy happiness – but it's more comfortable to cry in a Porsche than in a Skoda.

The Top Ten Men

1. The doctor because he says, 'Take your clothes off.'
2. The dentist because he says, 'Open wide.'
3. The hairdresser because he says, 'Do you want it teased or blown?'
4. The milkman because he says, 'Do you want it in the front or in the back?'
5. The interior decorator because he says, 'Once you have done it, you'll love it.'
6. The banker because he says, 'If you take it out too soon, you'll lose interest.'
7. The police officer because he says, 'Spread 'em.'
8. The mailman because he always delivers his package.
9. The pilot because he takes off fast and then slows down.
10. The hunter because he always goes deep in the bush and shoots it twice.

Talk about hitting the nail on the head:

WHAT DOES IT MEAN WHEN A MAN IS IN YOUR BED GASPING FOR BREATH AND CALLING YOUR NAME?
YOU DIDN'T HOLD THE PILLOW DOWN FOR LONG ENOUGH.

Why do only ten per cent of men make it to heaven?
Because if they all went, it would be HELL.

WHY DO MEN LIKE SMART WOMEN?
OPPOSITES ATTRACT.

How are men like lawn mowers?
They're hard to get started, they emit noxious odours
and half the time they don't work.

How do men define a 50/50 relationship?
We cook/they eat; we clean/they dirty; we iron/they wrinkle.

How do you get a man to stop biting his nails?
Make him wear shoes.

How many men does it take to screw in a light bulb?
One. He just holds it up and waits for the world to
revolve around him.

Why did God create man before woman?
Because you're always supposed to have
a rough draft before creating your
masterpiece.

Why do men play sports on artificial turf?
To keep them from grazing.

Why do men need instant replay on TV sports?
Because after thirty seconds they forgot what happened.

Why is psychoanalysis a lot quicker for men than women?
It takes no time to go back to his childhood — he's already there.

Written on the mirror in a women's lavatory:

IT'S A GOOD THING FOR YOU THAT MIRRORS CAN'T LAUGH.

And:

*You obviously have a lot of time on your hands
and the wrinkles to prove it.*

And also:

I'm told men drink to your face - they'd have to.

On husbands:

My husband is kind to his inferiors ... but what I want to know is, where does he find them?

My husband started at the bottom . . .and sank.

Judge a man not by his clothes, but by his wife's clothes.

**My husband gets lost in thought.
It is unfamiliar territory.**

`My husband has the face of a saint – a Saint Bernard.`

Drinking makes some husbands see double and feel single.

Tell your husband you like the 'lateral coital position' and then watch his face when you tell him it means 'a bit on the side'.

My ex-husband has a wonderful head on his shoulders ... a different one each night.

When a man scrawled:

What's the difference between a girlfriend and a wife? ... Four stones.

Underneath a woman added:

WHAT'S THE DIFFERENCE BETWEEN A BOYFRIEND AND A HUSBAND? ... FORTY-FIVE MINUTES.

WHAT ARE THE THREE WORDS GUARANTEED TO HUMILIATE MEN EVERYWHERE? ... 'HOLD MY PURSE.'

A thing you'll never hear a woman say:

'My, what an attractive scrotum!'

You know you are getting old when you put your bra on backwards - and it fits!

The best form of birth control after fifty is nudity.

How many women does it take to change a light bulb?
None, they just sit there in the dark and bitch.

Why men pee standing up

God is just about done creating man, but he has two items left in his bag and he can't quite decide how to split them between Adam and Eve. He thinks he might as well ask them. He tells them one of the things he has left is a thing that will allow the owner to pee while standing up. 'It's a very handy thing,' God tells them, 'and I was wondering if either one of you had a preference for it.'

Well, Adam gets excited and jumps up and down and begs, 'Oh, please give that to me! I'd love to be able to do that! It seems like just the sort of thing a man should have. Please! Please! Give it to me!' On and on he goes like an excited little boy.

Eve just smiles and tells God that if Adam really wants it so badly, he can have it. So God gives Adam the thing that allows him to pee standing up.

Adam is so excited he just starts pissing all over the place – first on the side of a rock, then he writes his name in the sand, and then he tries to see if he can hit a stump ten feet away – laughing with delight all the time.

God and Eve watch him with amusement and then God says to Eve, 'Well, you are left with the last thing I have in my bag. It is really very useful.'

'What's it called?' asks Eve.

'A Brain,' says God.

More questions and answers:

Why are men and parking spaces alike?
Because all the good ones are gone and the only ones left are disabled.

What have men and floor tiles got in common?
If you lay them properly the first time, you can
walk all over them for life.

WHY DO MEN WANT TO MARRY VIRGINS?
THEY CAN'T STAND CRITICISM.

Why is it so hard for women to find men who are
sensitive, caring, and good looking?
Because those men already have boyfriends.

What's the difference between a new husband and a
new dog?
After a year, the dog is still excited to see you.

What makes men chase women they have no
intention of marrying?
The same urge that makes dogs chase cars they
have no intention of driving.

MOTHERS HAVE MOTHER'S DAY, DADS HAVE FATHER'S
DAY, WHAT DO SINGLE LONELY GUYS HAVE?
PALM SUNDAY.

Did you hear about the Chinese couple who had a
retarded baby?
They named him Sum Ting Wong.

What do toilets, a clitoris, and an anniversary have in common?
Men miss them all.

WHY DO MEN FIND IT DIFFICULT TO MAKE EYE CONTACT?
BREASTS DON'T HAVE EYES.

I get enough exercise just pushing my luck.

How many roads must a man walk down, before
He admits he is lost?

What's the Cuban National Anthem?
Michael, Row the Boat ashore, Halleluiah.

What's the difference between an English zoo,
and a Chinese zoo?
*A Chinese zoo has a description of the animal
on the front of the cage, along with a recipe.*

One day while taking a stroll, a woman comes upon a
gentleman neighbour who has the most beautiful garden
full of huge red tomatoes. The woman asks the gentleman,

'What do you do to get your tomatoes so red?' The gentleman responds, 'Well, twice a day I stand in front of my tomato garden and expose myself, and my tomatoes turn red from blushing so much.'

Well, the woman is so impressed, she decides to try doing the same thing to her tomato garden to see if it will work. So twice a day for two weeks she exposes herself to her garden hoping for the best.

One day the gentleman is passing by and asks the woman, 'By the way, how did you make out? Did your tomatoes turn red?'

'No,' she replies, 'but my cucumbers are enormous.'

10 PEOPLE DESPERATE TO GET MARRIED . . .

1. For years now, she's been planning a runaway marriage with her boyfriend, but every time they plan, he runs away.
2. She prays every night, 'Dear Lord I don't ask a thing for myself; just send my parents a son-in-law.'
3. Even at a charity ball, men don't ask her to dance.
4. His father wanted a boy and his mother wanted a girl. They are both satisfied.
5. He asked a girl for, 'Just three little words that will make me walk on air.' She obliged him with, 'Go hang yourself.'
6. He says he can marry any girl he pleases ... The trouble is, he doesn't please anybody.

7. *For years he's been looking for a girl who's tall and willowy … Now he'll settle for one who's short and willing.*
8. *The boys don't call her attractive, nor do they call her homely; they just don't call her.*
9. *With those low-cut dresses it's obvious she's out to catch a man, but all she catches is a cold.*
10. *She was two-thirds married once … She was there, the minister was there, but the groom did not show up.*

At a White House press conference in 2000, Tipper Gore announces that she is going on the Presidential Campaign Trail with her husband, the then Vice President Al Gore. 'To prepare myself,' she says, 'I have shaved off all my pubic hair. From now until the election, I shall sit on the stage with the Vice President, and will have my legs apart without wearing any panties.'

'What is the message?' gasp the astonished reporters at the news of this startling announcement.

'Read my lips: No more Bush.'

Pinned up in the canteen of a department store:

Mr Mellor gets himself a new secretary. She is young, sweet and very polite. One day while taking dictation, she notices his fly is open.

When leaving the room, she says, 'Mr Mellor, your barracks door is open.'

He does not understand her remark, but later on he happens to look down and see that his zipper is undone. He decides to have some fun with his secretary, so calling her in, he enquires, 'By the way, Miss Jones, when you saw my barracks door was open this morning, did you also notice a soldier standing to attention?'

The secretary thinks for a moment and then replies, 'Why, no Mr Mellor, all I saw was a little, disabled veteran sitting on two duffel bags.'

I'M NOT OFFENDED BY ALL THE DUMB BLONDE JOKES BECAUSE I KNOW I'M NOT DUMB ... AND I ALSO KNOW THAT I'M NOT BLONDE.

Puritanism: *the haunting fear that someone, somewhere may be happy.*

Women are the cleverer sex. You see a lot of smart guys with dumb women, but you hardly ever see a smart woman with a dumb guy.

I want to have children, but I am scared. One of my friends told me she was in labour for 36 hours. I don't even want to do anything that feels good for 36 hours.

The cure for loneliness is solitude.

Money isn't everything, but it keeps the kids in touch.

The other day, my girlfriends and I go to this 'Ladies Night Club'. One of my friends wants to impress us, so she pulls out a ten-pound note. The 'male dancer' comes over to us, and my friend licks the ten-pound note and pastes it on his bum cheek.

Not to be outdone, another friend pulls out a twenty-pound note. She calls the guy back over, licks the £20 note and pastes that on his other buttock cheek.

Attempting to impress the rest of us, my other friend pulls out a fifty-pound note. She calls the guy back over again, licks the fifty-pound note and again pastes it on one of his buttock cheeks.

Now the attention is focused on me. What can I do to top that? I get out my purse, think for a minute ... and then the practical woman in me takes over. I get out my ACCESS card, swipe it down the crack of his arse, grab the eighty pounds cash and go home.

A notice was recently seen pinned up at a secretarial college:

RULES FOR WOMEN

Rule 1.   Never lend your car to anyone to whom you have given birth.

Rule 2.   If high heels were so wonderful, men would be wearing them.

Rule 3.   Deciding 'what is fashionable' is easy.
          Just wear something that doesn't itch.

Rule 4.   You will never hear a man ask for advice
          on how to combine marriage and a career.

Rule 5.   Never marry – and if you get the urge to,
          just buy three pets; a dog, a parrot and a
          cat. They'll serve the same purpose as a
          husband. The dog will growl every
          morning. The parrot will swear all
          afternoon and the cat will come home
          late most nights.

Rule 6.   When accused of nagging, just remember
          that nagging is only the repetition of
          unpalatable truths.

Some graffiti entitled 'Historical Facts':

Abraham Lincoln was elected to Congress in 1846.
John F Kennedy was elected to Congress in 1946.
Abraham Lincoln was elected President in 1860.
John F Kennedy was elected President in 1960.
The names Lincoln and Kennedy each contain seven letters.
Both were particularly concerned with civil rights.
Both wives lost children while living in the White House.
Both Presidents were shot on a Friday.
Both Presidents were shot in the head.
Lincoln's secretary was named Kennedy.
Kennedy's secretary was named Lincoln.
Both were assassinated by Southerners.
Both were succeeded by Southerners.
Both successors were named Johnson.
Andrew Johnson, who succeeded Lincoln, was born in 1808.
Lyndon Johnson, who succeeded Kennedy, was born in 1908.

John Wilkes Booth, who assassinated Lincoln, was born in 1839.

Lee Harvey Oswald, who assassinated Kennedy, was born in 1939.

Both assassins were known by their three names.

Both names are comprised of fifteen letters.

Lincoln was shot at the theatre named 'Kennedy'.

Kennedy was shot in a car called a 'Lincoln'.

Booth ran from the theatre and was caught in a warehouse.

Oswald ran from a warehouse and was caught in a theatre.

Booth and Oswald were assassinated before their trials.

And here's the most surprising fact ...

A week before Lincoln was shot, he was in Monroe, Maryland.

A week before Kennedy was shot, he was in Monroe, Marilyn!

I just broke up with my boyfriend and the last thing he said to me was, 'You'll never find anyone like me again!' Well, I should hope not! If I don't want him, why would I want someone like him?

EUSTACE FLAHERTY DIES IN A FIRE AND HIS BODY IS VERY BADLY BURNT. THE MORGUE NEEDS SOMEONE TO IDENTIFY THE BODY, SO HIS TWO BEST FRIENDS, PADDY AND SHEAMUS, ARE SENT FOR.

PADDY GOES IN AND THE MORTICIAN PULLS BACK THE SHEET. PADDY SAYS, 'YUP, HE'S BURNT PRETTY BAD. ROLL HIM OVER.'

THE MORTICIAN ROLLS HIM OVER, AND PADDY SAYS, 'NOPE, AIN'T EUSTACE.'

THE MORTICIAN THINKS THAT IS RATHER STRANGE. THEN HE BRINGS SHEAMUS IN TO IDENTIFY THE BODY. SHEAMUS

TAKES A LOOK AT HIM AND SAYS, 'YUP, HE'S BURNT REAL BAD, ROLL HIM OVER.'

THE MORTICIAN ROLLS HIM OVER AND SHEAMUS SAYS, 'NO, IT AIN'T EUSTACE.'

THE MORTICIAN ASKS, 'HOW CAN YOU TELL?'

SHEAMUS SAYS, 'WELL, EUSTACE HAD TWO ARSEHOLES.'

'WHAT? HE HAD TWO ARSEHOLES?' SAYS THE MORTICIAN.

'YUP, EVERYONE IN TOWN KNEW HE HAD TWO ARSEHOLES. EVERYTIME WE WENT TO TOWN WITH HIM FOLKS WOULD SAY, "HERE COMES EUSTACE WITH THEM TWO ARSEHOLES."'

Don't spend five quid to dry clean your husband's shirt.
Donate it to the Salvation Army instead.
They'll clean it and put it on a hanger.
Next morning go into their shop and buy it back for one pound fifty.

Shin: *a device for finding furniture in the dark.*

Some people are only alive because it is illegal to shoot them.

Women who seek to be equal to men lack ambition.

Your gene pool could use some chlorine.

> *Change is inevitable, except from a vending machine*

An accountant decides to leave his wife one day. He leaves her a note saying: 'Dear Jane, I am fifty-four years old and I have never done anything wild. So I'm leaving you for an eighteen-year-old blonde model. We'll be staying at the Sheraton.' He then packs his things and goes there.

When he arrives at the Sheraton, there is a message for him from his wife. It reads: 'Dear John. I too am fifty-four years old. I have followed your example and am staying at the Hyatt with an eighteen-year-old Italian hunk. And I'm sure that you, as an accountant, will appreciate that eighteen goes into fifty-four many many more times than fifty-four goes into eighteen!'

For a Buddhist monk, chants is a fine thing.

Caution – Essex girl thinking.

Lottery: A tax on people who are bad at maths.

Never underestimate the power of stupid people in large groups.

Schizophrenia beats being alone.

Suicidal twin kills sister by mistake!

WEAR SHORT SLEEVES . . . SUPPORT YOUR RIGHT TO BARE ARMS!

They call it PMS because
'Mad Cow Disease' was already taken.

When blondes have more fun, do they know it?

I was married by a judge. I should have asked for a jury!

All men are animals — some just make better pets.

Not all graffiti is unpleasant:

It takes a minute to have a crush on someone, an hour to like someone and a day to love someone – but it takes a lifetime to forget someone.

Real friends are those who, when you feel you've made a fool of yourself, don't feel you've done a permanent job.

To the world you might be one person, but to one person you might be the world.

I used to have a handle on life but it broke.

A woman gives birth to a baby. Afterwards, the doctor comes in, and he says to her, 'I have to tell you something about your baby.'

At this the woman becomes concerned. She sits up in bed and says, 'What's wrong with my baby, Doctor? What's wrong???'

The doctor says, 'Well, now, nothing's wrong, exactly, but your baby is a little bit different. Your baby is a hermaphrodite.'

The woman says, 'A hermaphrodite ... what's that???'

The doctor says, 'Well, it means your baby has the ... er ... features ... of a male and a female.'

The woman turns pale. She says, 'Oh my God! You mean it has a penis . . . AND a brain?'

DON'T LEND MONEY - IT CAUSES AMNESIA.

What's the difference between in-laws and outlaws?
Outlaws are wanted!

25 signs you are growing old

1. Your houseplants are alive, and you can't smoke any of them.
2. Having sex in a single bed is out of the question.
3. You keep more vitamin pills than wine in the house.
4. Six in the morning is when you get up, not when you go to bed.

5. You hear your favourite song being played in a lift.
6. You watch the Weather Channel.
7. Your friends marry and divorce instead of living together.
8. You go from 21 days of holiday time to 365.
9. Jeans and a sweater no longer qualify as 'dressed up'.
10. You're the one calling the police because those bloody kids next door won't turn down their stereo.
11. When you walk into a bar, the barman asks if you want a glass of Wincarnis.
12. You don't know what time McDonald's closes anymore.
13. Your car insurance goes down and your car payments go up.
14. You feed your dog Science Diet instead of McDonald's leftovers.
15. Sleeping on a couch makes your back hurt.
16. You take afternoon naps.
17. Dinner and a movie is the whole date instead of the beginning of one.
18. Eating a basket of chicken wings at two in the morning severely upsets, rather than settles, your stomach.
19. You go to the chemists for philosan and antacid, not condoms and pregnancy tests.
20. A two-pound bottle of wine no longer tastes 'pretty good stuff'.
21. You actually eat breakfast food at breakfast time.
22. 'I just can't drink the way I used to,' replaces, 'I'm never going to drink that much again.'
23. Ninety per cent of the time you spend in front of a computer is for real work.
24. You drink at home to save money before going to a bar.
25. You read this entire list looking for a couple of signs that don't apply to you and can't find one. Then you forward it to a group of friends because you know they'll do the same . . .

If sex is a pain in the arse, then you're doing it wrong ...

All men are idiots, and I married their king.

THE SCOTS ARE LIKE HAEMORRHOIDS ...
IF THEY COME DOWN AND GO BACK UP, NO PROBLEM.
IT'S WHEN THEY COME DOWN AND STAY DOWN THAT THEY'RE A PAIN IN THE ARSE.

Some more philosophy:

Always remember you're unique, just like everyone else.

Always try to be modest and be proud of it.

Give a man a fish and he will eat for a day. Teach him how to fish, and he will sit in a boat drinking beer all day.

If at first you don't succeed, destroy all evidence that you tried.

I'm not a complete idiot; some parts are missing.

Some advice for women seen scrawled on a sign pinned up at a nightclub:

Women's unwanted pick-up line comebacks

Man: 'Haven't we met before?'   LUNATIC ASYLUM
Woman: 'Yes, I'm the receptionist at the VD Clinic.'

Man: 'Haven't I seen you someplace before?'
Woman: 'Yeah, that's why I don't go there anymore.'

Man: 'Is this seat empty?'
Woman: 'Yes, and this one will be too if you sit down.'

Man: 'So, wanna go back to my place ?'
Woman: 'Well, I don't know. Will two people fit under a rock?'

Man: 'Your place or mine?'
Woman: 'Both. You go to yours and I'll go to mine.'

Man: 'I'd like to call you. What's your number?'
Woman: 'It's in the phone book.'

Man: 'But I don't know your name.'
Woman: 'That's in the phone book too.'

Man: 'So what do you do for a living?'
Woman: 'I'm a female impersonator.'

Man: 'What sign were you born under?'
Woman: 'No Parking.'

Man: 'Hey, baby, what's your sign?'
Woman: 'Do Not Enter.'

Man: 'How do you like your eggs in the morning?'
Woman: 'Unfertilised!'

Man: 'Hey, come on, we're both here at this bar for the same reason.'
Woman: 'Yeah! Let's pick up some chicks!'

Man: 'I'm here to fulfill your every sexual fantasy.'
Woman: 'You mean you've got both a donkey and a Great Dane?'

Man: 'I know how to please a woman.'
Woman: 'Then please leave me alone.'

Man: 'I want to give myself to you.'
Woman: 'Sorry, I don't accept cheap gifts.'

Man: 'I can tell that you want me.'
Woman: 'You're so right. I want you to leave.'

Man: 'If I could see you naked, I'd die happy.'
Woman: 'Yes, but if I saw you naked, I'd die laughing.'

Man: 'Hey cutie, how 'bout you and I hitting the hot spots?'
Woman: 'Sorry, I don't date outside my species.'

Man: 'Your body is like a temple.'
Woman: 'Sorry, there are no services today.'

Man: 'I'd go through anything for you.'
Woman: 'Good! Let's start with your bank account.'

Man: 'I would go to the end of the world for you.'
Woman: 'Good, but would you stay there?'

Sex is like air - it's not important unless you aren't getting any.

LAST NIGHT SEX WAS SO GOOD THAT EVEN THE NEIGHBOURS HAD A CIGARETTE.

And finally in this section:

If men can really run the world, why can't they stop wearing ties? How can any intelligent person start the day by tying a little noose around his neck?

3

ALL THOSE OTHER PLACES

When someone scrawled on the wall of a disused church:

And God said: 'Let there be Satan, so people don't blame everything on Me.'

Some wag added underneath:

And let there be lawyers, so people don't blame everything on Satan.

A woman wrote the following quote on a unisex lavatory at a café and thought it was GREAT!:

Men are like fine wine. They all start out like grapes, and it's our job to stomp on them and keep them in the dark until they mature into something with which you'd like to have dinner.

As you might expect, it was not long before a man countered this quote and scrawled underneath:

But women are also like fine wine.
They all start out fresh, fruity and intoxicating
to the mind and then turn full-bodied with age
until they go all sour and vinegary and give you
a flaming headache.

So, the battle of the sexes continues.

Before the collapse of the USSR, former British Member of Parliament John M Taylor had occasion to visit the Berlin Wall. He was amazed at the extent of the graffiti daubed on this symbol of Eastern bloc repression. He found himself scanning the scrawlings to find something written in English. Eventually, his eyes lit upon the words:

`Geoff Boycott - we love you.`

He continued his trip and then returned to Britain, where the following evening he was the guest speaker at a function organised by his local cricket club.

During the course of giving his views on world events he mentioned the very moving experience he had had visiting the Berlin Wall and added how he had searched the graffiti for some message written in English. He explained to them how the first intelligible sentence he had seen was, 'Geoff Boycott - we love you'.

On hearing this, some wag at the back of the room shouted out: 'Which side of the wall was it written on?'

It was at that point he felt he started to lose his audience.

Written on the back of a truck in the USA during the 2004 Presidential election:

BUSH-CHENEY – FOUR MORE WARS.

After the 2003 Iraqi defeat by the coalition forces, which toppled Saddam Hussein, the following was seen scrawled on a wall at a building site:

Free hardcore, phone Baghdad 3699.

Seen on the back of a grubby white van:

I wish my wife was as dirty as this.

And on the back of another white van:

Lost - wife and dog.
Reward for dog.

On the lavatory wall in a hotel function room:

If you are saying grace tonight try this one:

Oh Lord please bless this food and wine,
And those here present about to dine,
But if long speeches we must endure,
Pray God they serve a good liqueur.

Someone faced with a lively rugby club audience, might, however, prefer the grace told by the late ventriloquist Arthur Worsley:

Thank you Lord for everything,
The food, the wine and all,
Thank you for all creatures,
be they great or small.
And if I should return to earth,
within this self-same figure,
Please Lord, leave me as I am,
but with my penis six inches bigger.

Seen on a noticeboard in a training hospital:

A Scotsman is in hospital and when lunch comes round he lifts the lid on his plate to find haggis, neeps and tatties. He is quite happy as he enjoys haggis. Tea time comes and again when he lifts the lid there is haggis, neeps and tatties. He isn't too bothered as he enjoys haggis so he says nothing.

Next day at lunchtime, once again – haggis, neeps and tatties. He is getting a bit fed up but still says nothing. At teatime he sees haggis, neeps and tatties on his plate again. This time he loses his cool and rings for the nurse.

'Anything wrong?' she says.

'Yes,' he says, 'this is the fourth time I have had haggis, neeps and tatties and I'm fed up with it.'

'What do you expect?' says the nurse, 'You are in the *Burns* unit.'

Jokes about 'Essex Girls' were very common in the 1970s and 1980s, and the quips have not gone away. Grossly unfair and insulting, the following have been seen scrawled on bus shelters, lavatories and elsewhere:

What does the label in an Essex girl's knickers say?
NEXT.

Why aren't Essex girls allowed coffee breaks?
Because it takes too long to retrain them.

What do you call an Essex girl with two brain cells?
Pregnant.

Why did the Essex girl scale the glass wall?
To see what was on the other side.

What is the difference between an Essex girl and the Grand Old Duke of York?
The Grand Old Duke of York only had ten thousand men.

How do you know an Essex girl has been using a computer?
There is Tippex all over the screen.

What do you call a fly buzzing inside an Essex girl's head?
A space invader.

How does an Essex girl know which way to put her knickers on?

She buys them at C and A.

How does an Essex girl turn the light out after sex?

She just shuts the car door.

How do you amuse an Essex girl for several hours?

Just write 'please turn over' on both sides of a piece of paper.

Why do all Essex girls fancy VW cars?

Because they can't spell Porsche.

What do you call an Essex girl with an IQ of 250?

Basildon.

What is the only thing that an Essex girl can put behind her ears to make her more attractive?

Her ankles.

WHAT DO YOU CALL AN ESSEX GIRL BEHIND A STEERING WHEEL?
AN AIRBAG.

What is the similarity between an Essex girl and a beer bottle?

They are both empty from the neck up.

How do you make an Essex girl laugh every Saturday?

Tell her a joke every Wednesday.

What's the difference between an Essex girl and a walrus?
One has whiskers and smells of fish – the other is a walrus.

What does an Essex girl say after she graduates?

Hi, welcome to McDonald's. '

What do you call an Essex blonde's skeleton in the closet?
Last year's hide and seek champ.

What do you call an Essex blonde with half a brain? Gifted.

How do Essex blondes' brain cells die? Alone.

Why did the Essex blonde resolve to have only three children?
Because she read that one child out of every four born was Chinese.

What do you call it when an Essex blonde dyes her hair brunette?
Artificial intelligence.

How do you make an Essex girl's eyes sparkle?
Shine a torch in her ear.

What does the left leg of an Essex blonde say to her right leg?
Nothing. They have never met.

And still more:

Have you heard about the Essex girl hurt in a car crash? The
ambulanceman asked her, 'Where are you bleeding from?'
The reply was: 'I am from bleeding Harlow.'

If you had fifteen Essex girls standing in a circle would
this be a dope ring?

Essex girls don't breastfeed their babies
because it's too painful to boil their nipples.

And finally, to provide some sexual balance here:

Did you hear about the Essex man who had eight
vasectomies? ...
He said he had to – his wife kept getting pregnant!

It says in the Bible that a man should
always make the tea. (Hebrews)

On the college wall:

I almost had a psychic girlfriend but she left me
before we met.

Some burning questions:

OK, SO WHAT'S THE SPEED OF DARK?

How do you tell when you're out of invisible ink?

If one synchronised swimmer drowns, do the rest have to drown too?

WHY DO WOMEN WEAR EVENING GOWNS TO NIGHTCLUBS? SHOULDN'T THEY BE WEARING NIGHTGOWNS?

Do paranoid schizophrenic agnostic dyslexic insomniacs lie awake at night wondering if they might be the dog that's out to get them?

What happens if you get scared half to death twice?

When the inventor of the drawing board messed up what did he go back to?

Why do psychics have to ask you for your name?

A LIGHT AT THE END OF THE TUNNEL
A TRAIN COMING TO-WARDS YOU

And more philosophy:

If everything seems to be going well, you have obviously overlooked something.

Depression is merely anger without enthusiasm.

When everything is coming your way, you're in the wrong lane.

Ambition is a poor excuse for not having enough sense to be lazy.

Hard work pays off in the future. Laziness pays off now.

My pet's a doughnut — a sweet-toothed canine.

Sign in pet store:

Buy one dog at the regular price, and get one flea ...

Everyone has a photographic memory; some just don't have film.

I intend to live forever — so far, so good.

24 hours in a day ... 24 beers in a case ... that's no coincidence.

I am grateful that I am not as judgmental as all those censorious, self-righteous bastards around me.

WHEN I'M NOT IN MY RIGHT MIND, MY LEFT MIND GETS PRETTY CROWDED.

I used to have an open mind but my brains kept falling out.

Riding the favourite at Cheltenham, a jockey is well ahead of the field. Suddenly he is hit on the head by a turkey and a string of sausages. He manages to keep control of his mount and pulls back into the lead, only to be struck by a box of Christmas crackers and a dozen mince pies as he goes over the last fence. With great skill he manages to steer the horse to the front of the field once more when, on the run in, he is struck on the head by a bottle of sherry and a Christmas pudding. Thus distracted, he succeeds in coming only second. He immediately goes to the stewards to complain that ...

Wait for it ...

He had been seriously hampered.

My girlfriend has a figure like a pepper-pot . . .
Does she take that as a condiment?

Pinned on a blackboard in the religious education class:

One Sunday morning during service, a two thousand member congregation is surprised to see two men enter, both covered from head to toe in black and carrying sub-machine guns. One of the men proclaims, 'Anyone willing to take a bullet for Christ remain where you are.'

Immediately, the choir flee, the deacons flee, and most of the congregation flee. Out of the two thousand originally there, there only remain around twenty people.

The man who had spoken takes off his hood, looks at the preacher and says, 'Okay Pastor, I got rid of all the hypocrites. Now you may begin your service. Have a nice day!'

And the two men turn and walk out.

And two more tall tales:

Four surgeons are taking a coffee break and discussing their work. The first says, 'I think accountants are the easiest to operate on. You open them up and everything inside is numbered.'

The second says, 'I think librarians are the easiest to operate on. You open them up and everything inside is in alphabetical order.'

The third says, 'I like to operate on electricians. You open them up and everything inside is colour coded.'

The fourth one says, 'I prefer to operate on New Labour MPs. They're heartless, spineless, gutless; and their heads and behinds are interchangeable.'

An elderly couple are holidaying in the American Mid-West. Arnold always wanted a pair of authentic cowboy boots so seeing some on sale one day, he buys them and wears them back to his hotel, walking proudly. He walks into their room and says to his wife, 'Notice anything different, Elsie?'

Elsie looks him over, 'Nope.'

Arnold says excitedly, 'Come on, Elsie, take a good look. Notice anything different about me?'

Elsie looks again. 'Nope.'

Frustrated, Arnold storms off into the bathroom, undresses, and walks back into the room completely naked except for his boots. Again, he asks, a little louder this time, 'Notice anything DIFFERENT?'

Elsie looks up and says, 'Arnold, what's different? It's hanging down today, it was hanging down yesterday, it'll be hanging down again tomorrow.'

Furious, Arnold yells, 'AND DO YOU KNOW WHY IT IS HANGING DOWN, ELSIE? IT'S HANGING DOWN BECAUSE IT'S LOOKING AT MY NEW BOOTS!!!'

To which Elsie replies, 'Shoulda bought a hat, Arnold. You shoulda bought a hat ...'

Every morning is the dawn of a new error.

If you always take time to stop and smell the roses - sooner or later, you'll inhale a bee.

IN ORDER TO KEEP A TRUE PERSPECTIVE OF ONE'S IMPORTANCE, EVERYONE SHOULD HAVE A DOG THAT WILL WORSHIP HIM AND A CAT THAT WILL IGNORE HIM.

It is now beyond any doubt that cigarettes are the biggest cause of statistics.

This is a supposed bricklayer's accident report, posted up on a noticeboard in a building site hut. It is claimed it is a true story:

Dear Sir

I am writing in response to your request for additional information in Block 3 of the accident report form. I put 'Poor planning' as the cause of my accident. You asked for a fuller explanation and I trust the following details will be sufficient.

I am a bricklayer by trade. On the day of the accident, I was working alone on the roof of a new six-storey building. When I completed my work, I found I had some bricks left over, which when weighed later were found to be slightly in excess of 500lb.

Rather than carry the bricks down by hand, I decided to lower them in a barrel by using a pulley, which was attached to the side of the building on the sixth floor.

Securing the rope at ground level, I went up to the roof, swung the barrel out and loaded the bricks into it. Then I went down and untied the rope, holding it tightly to ensure a slow descent of the bricks. You will note in Block 11 of the accident report form that I weigh 135lb.

Due to my surprise at being jerked off the ground so suddenly, I lost my presence of mind and forgot to let go of the rope. Needless to say, I proceeded at a rapid rate up the side of the building.

In the vicinity of the third floor, I met the barrel which was now proceeding downward at an impressive speed. This explains the fractured skull, minor abrasions and the broken collarbone, as listed in Section 3 of the accident report form. Slowed only slightly by the bricks, I continued my rapid ascent, not stopping until the fingers of my right hand were two knuckles deep into the pulley.

Fortunately by this time I had regained my presence of mind and was able to hold tightly to the rope, in spite of the excruciating pain I was now beginning to experience. At approximately the same time, however, the barrel of bricks hit the ground and the bottom fell out of the barrel.

Devoid of the weight of the bricks, that barrel now weighed only approximately 50lb. I refer you again to my weight. As you might imagine, I began a rapid descent, down the side of the building.

In the vicinity of the third floor, I met the barrel coming up. This accounts for the two fractured ankles, broken tooth and severe lacerations of my legs and lower body.

Here my luck began to change slightly. The encounter with the barrel seemed to slow me enough to lessen my injuries when I fell into the pile of bricks on the ground and fortunately only three vertebrae were cracked.

I am sorry to report, however, as I lay there on the pile of bricks, in pain, unable to move, I again lost my presence of mind and I let go of the rope. As I lay there, the empty barrel began its journey back down onto me. This explains the two broken legs.

I hope this answers your enquiry.

Amusing yes, but an unlikely 'true story'. The tale is almost identical to the humorous speech often made in the UK by the late raconteur, Gerard Hoffnung, which was recorded and released as a record in the early 1960s.

One day, in line at the company cafeteria, Jack says to Mike behind him, 'My elbow hurts like hell. I guess I better see a doctor.'

'Listen, you don't have to spend that kind of money,' Mike replies. 'There's a diagnostic computer at the drugstore at the corner. Just give it a urine sample and the computer will tell you what's wrong and what to do about it. It takes ten seconds and costs ten dollars ... a hell of a lot cheaper than a doctor.'

So Jack deposits a urine sample in a small jar and

takes it to the drugstore. He deposits ten dollars, and the computer lights up and asks for the urine sample. He pours the sample into the slot and waits. Ten seconds later, the computer ejects a printout:

You have tennis elbow. Soak your arm in warm water and avoid heavy activity. It will improve in two weeks.

That evening while thinking how amazing this new technology was, Jack begins wondering if the computer could be fooled. He mixes some tap water, a stool sample from his dog, urine samples from his wife and daughter, and masturbates into the mixture for good measure.

Jack hurries back to the drugstore, eager to check the results. He deposits ten dollars, pours in his concoction, and awaits the results. The computer prints the following:

1. *Your tap water is too hard. Get a water softener.*
2. *Your dog has ringworm. Bathe him with anti-fungal shampoo.*
3. *Your daughter has a cocaine habit. Get her into rehab.*
4. *Your wife is pregnant . . . twin girls. They aren't yours. Get a lawyer.*
5. *And, if you don't stop playing with yourself, your elbow will never get better.*

UK ARMY
OFFICIAL VOICEMAIL MESSAGE

THANK YOU FOR CALLING THE BRITISH ARMY. I'M SORRY, BUT ALL OF OUR UNITS ARE OUT AT THE MOMENT, OR ARE OTHERWISE ENGAGED. PLEASE LEAVE A MESSAGE WITH DETAILS OF YOUR COUNTRY, NAME OF ORGANISATION, THE REGION, THE SPECIFIC CRISIS, AND A NUMBER AT WHICH WE CAN CALL YOU. AS SOON AS WE HAVE SORTED OUT THE BALKANS, IRAQ, NORTHERN IRELAND, AFGHANISTAN, MARCHING UP AND DOWN BITS OF TARMAC IN LONDON AND OUR NOW COMPULSORY EQUAL OPPORTUNITIES TRAINING, WE WILL RETURN YOUR CALL. PLEASE SPEAK AFTER THE TONE, OR IF YOU REQUIRE MORE OPTIONS, PLEASE LISTEN TO THE FOLLOWING NUMBERS:

IF YOUR CRISIS IS SMALL, AND CLOSE TO THE SEA:
PRESS 1 FOR THE *ROYAL MARINES*.
IF YOUR CONCERN IS DISTANT, WITH A TROPICAL CLIMATE AND GOOD HOTELS, AND CAN BE SOLVED BY ONE OR TWO LOW RISK BOMBING RUNS,
PLEASE PRESS HASH FOR THE *ROYAL AIR FORCE*.
PLEASE NOTE THIS SERVICE IS NOT AVAILABLE AFTER 1630 HOURS, OR AT WEEKENDS.
IF YOUR ENQUIRY CONCERNS A SITUATION WHICH CAN BE RESOLVED BY A BIT OF GREY FUNNEL, BUNTING, FLAGS AND A REALLY GOOD MARCHING BAND, PLEASE WRITE, WELL IN ADVANCE, TO THE *FIRST SEA LORD*, THE ADMIRALTY, WHITEHALL.
IF YOUR ENQUIRY IS NOT URGENT, PLEASE PRESS 2 FOR THE *ALLIED RAPID REACTION CORPS*.
IF YOU ARE IN REAL, HOT TROUBLE PLEASE PRESS 3 AND YOUR CALL WILL BE ROUTED TO THE US EMBASSY.

IF YOU ARE INTERESTED IN JOINING THE BRITISH ARMY AND WISH TO BE SHOUTED AT, PAID LITTLE, HAVE PREMATURE ARTHRITIS, HAVE YOUR WIFE AND FAMILY PLACED IN A CONDEMNED HOVEL MILES FROM CIVILISATION, AND ARE PREPARED TO WORK YOUR ARSE OFF DAILY, RISKING YOUR LIFE, IN ALL WEATHERS AND TERRAINS, BOTH DAY AND NIGHT, WHILST WATCHING HM TREASURY ERODING YOUR ORIGINAL TERMS AND CONDITIONS OF SERVICE, THEN PLEASE STAY ON THE LINE. YOUR CALL WILL SHORTLY BE CONNECTED TO A BITTER PASSED-OVER RECRUITING SERGEANT IN A GROTTY SHOP DOWN BY THE RAILWAY STATION.
HAVE A PLEASANT DAY, AND THANK YOU AGAIN FOR TRYING TO CONTACT THE BRITISH ARMY.

Nothing is impossible to those who don't have to do it.

Pinned up in a US post office:

SUBJECT: WATCH WHAT U LICK IF YOU LICK YOUR ENVELOPES . . . YOU WON'T ANYMORE!

A woman was working in a post office in California. One day she licked the envelopes and postage stamps instead of using a sponge. That very day the lady cut her tongue on the envelope. A week later, she noticed an abnormal swelling of her tongue. She went to the doctor, and they found nothing wrong. Her tongue was not sore nor was there any known symptoms.

However, two days later, her tongue started to swell more and it began to get really sore; so sore that she could not eat. She went back to the hospital, and demanded something be done. The doctor took an X-ray of her tongue, and noticed a lump. He prepared her for minor surgery.

When the doctor cut her tongue open, a live cockroach crawled out. There were cockroach eggs on the seal of the envelope. The egg was able to hatch inside of her tongue because of her saliva. It was warm and moist.

(This is a true story reported on CNN!)

Hey, I used to work in an envelope factory. You wouldn't believe the things that float around in those gum applicator trays. I haven't licked an envelope for years.

Andy

On a club noticeboard:

THE WORST THINGS TO SAY TO A POLICE OFFICER

'I can't reach my licence unless you hold my beer.'
'Sorry, Officer, I didn't realise my radar detector wasn't plugged in.'
'Aren't you the guy from the Village People?'
'Hey, you must've been doin' about 125 mph to keep up with me!'
'I thought you had to be in good physical condition to be a police officer.'
'I was going to be a cop, but I decided to finish high school instead.'

'You're not gonna look in the boot, are you?'

'Goodness, that gut sure doesn't inspire confidence.'

'Didn't I see you get your arse kicked on *The Bill*?'

'Is it true that people become cops because they are too dumb to work at McDonald's?'

'I pay your salary!'

'That's terrific. The last officer only gave me a warning, too!'

'Do you know why you pulled me over? Okay, just so one of us does.'

'I was trying to keep up with traffic. Yes, I know there is no other car around – that's how far ahead of me they are.'

'What do you mean, "Have I been drinking?" You're the trained specialist.'

'Well, when I reached down to pick up my bag of crack, my gun fell off my lap and got lodged between the brake pedal and the accelerator pedal, forcing me to speed and go out of control.'

'Hi Honky Tonk, can you give me another one of those full cavity searches, ducky?'

Some wise words:

IF YOU MUST CHOOSE BETWEEN TWO EVILS, PICK THE ONE YOU'VE NEVER TRIED BEFORE.

If at first you don't succeed, then skydiving definitely isn't for you.

A conclusion is the place where you got tired of thinking.

Experience is something you don't get until just after you need it.

Age is a very high price to pay for maturity.

IF YOU THINK NOBODY CARES ABOUT YOU, TRY MISSING A COUPLE OF PAYMENTS.

Drugs may lead to nowhere, but at least it's the scenic route.

Borrow money from pessimists - they don't expect it back.

To be intoxicated is to feel sophisticated, but not be able to say it.

If lawyers are disbarred and clergymen defrocked, doesn't it follow that electricians can be delighted, musicians denoted, cowboys deranged, models deposed, tree surgeons debarked, and dry cleaners depressed?'

Half the people you know are below average.

All those who believe in telekinesis raise my hand.

A person reviewing people in an insane asylum walks around and is pleased with what he sees. He starts to review patients to see what they will do when they get out.

He walks up to the first guy and sees him throwing a football around. He automatically knows that he wants to be a football player.

He walks up to another guy and sees him throwing a baseball around. He can automatically tell that he wants to be a baseball player.

He walks to the next cell and sees a man with his private parts in a bowl of peanuts. He scratches his head and asks the man what he is doing. The man replies, 'I'm f***ing nuts. I'm never getting out of here!'

A blonde and a brunette are in a lift, when suddenly a good-looking handsome man gets in. The brunette turns to the blonde and says, 'Wow, he is so good looking, but that dandruff on him is a real turn off. I think we should give him some Head and Shoulders!'

The blonde looks at the brunette with a confused look and says, 'OK, but how do you give *shoulders*?'

On going to war over religion:

You're basically killing each other to see who's got the better imaginary friend.

And more burning questions:

IF A PIG LOSES ITS VOICE, IS IT DISGRUNTLED?

Are trendy left-wingers and pacifists violently opposed to the use of fur in clothing rather than leather because it's much easier to harass rich women than motorcycle gangs?

Where do the homeless have ninety per cent of their accidents?

What was the best thing before sliced bread?

What do gardeners do when they retire?

If you ate pasta and antipasta, would you still be hungry?

WHAT IF THERE WERE NO HYPOTHETICAL QUESTIONS?

Why is it that when we bounce a cheque, the bank charges us more of what they already know we don't have any of?

If you take an Oriental person and spin him around several times, would he become disoriented?

Is it possible to be totally partial?

Why is it that if the teacher tells you that there are one billion stars in the universe you will believe him, but if he tells you a wall has wet paint you still have to touch it to be sure?

Is there another word for synonym?

What's another word for thesaurus?

HOW CAN THERE BE SELF-HELP 'GROUPS'?

For Sale: Parachute. Only used once, never opened, small stain.

WHEN YOU LOOK AT PRINCE CHARLES, DON'T YOU THINK THAT SOMEONE IN THE ROYAL FAMILY KNEW SOMEONE IN THE ROYLE FAMILY?

Your girlfriend breaks up with you and sends you pictures of her and her new boyfriend in bed together.
Solution? Send them to her dad.

The statistics on sanity are that one out of every five Britons is suffering from some form of mental illness ... Think of your four best friends. If they're okay, then it's you.

Despite the take-over of Skoda cars by VW, the graffiti gibes against the marque continue with no sign of the trend abating:

What do you call a Skoda at the top of a hill?
A bloody miracle.

What do you call a Skoda with a seatbelt?
A rucksack.

What's the difference between a Skoda and a dress worn by Kate Moss?
You get a tit in a Skoda.

What do you call a Skoda with twin exhausts?
A wheelbarrow.

What do you call a Skoda with a sun roof?
A skip.

What do you call a Skoda with a radio aerial?
A dodgem.

WHY DO SKODAS HAVE HEATED REAR WINDOWS?
TO KEEP YOUR HANDS WARM WHEN YOU ARE PUSHING IT.

How do you treble the value of a Skoda in Britain?
Fill it with petrol.

How do you double the value of a Skoda in Poland?
Put a sack of potatoes in the boot.

How do you get a Skoda to go faster than a Jaguar?
Push it over the cliff first.

What is the difference between a Skoda and a sheep?
You feel rather less embarrassed being seen getting into the back of a sheep.

What information is contained in a Skoda
Owner's Manual?
A bus timetable.

What do you call someone who puts
sports stripes on the side of his
Skoda?
A prat.

How do you get your Skoda to go at over 55 mph?
Drive it over the White Cliffs of Dover.

How do you overtake a Skoda?
Easy. Just keep walking.

What is the difference between a Skoda and a
Barry Manilow concert?
Tickets for Barry Manilow go easy.

What is the difference between a Skoda and a golf ball?
You can drive a golf ball 100 yards.

Why do Skodas have two spare wheels?
So you can cycle home.

What do you call a Skoda with a turbo?
A blender.

HOW DO YOU MAKE A REALLY OLD SKODA
LOOK GOOD?
PARK IT NEXT TO TWO NEW ONES.

How do you make a Skoda disappear?
Apply rust remover.

What do you call the shock absorbers inside a
Skoda? Passengers.

What do you call a Skoda with a flat tyre?
A write-off.

How do you get a 16-valve Skoda?
Fit an old 12-valve radio.

Seen on a wall in an MOT testing station:

How do you economically repair a Skoda
MOT failure?
Remove the radiator cap, push the car over a
cliff. Tow in a brand-new Skoda, tighten the
radiator cap, and send the drippy owner the bill.

Overheard at a garage:

'Have you got a new petrol cap for my Skoda?'
Attendant (seriously): 'Well, yes. That seems like
a fair swap to me.'

... Here is the news. Two youths in a Skoda were arrested last night in London following a push-by shooting incident.

Did you hear about the Skoda owner who was stopped for speeding ... then he woke up.

And, the graffiti item that sums this section up:

What is the smallest part of a Skoda?
The owner's brain.

I met a Dutch girl with inflatable shoes last week, phoned her up to arrange a date but unfortunately she'd popped her clogs.

I'm against hunting. I'm a hunt saboteur.
I go out the night before and shoot the fox.

I've got a friend who's fallen in love with two schoolbags - he's bi-satchel.

I once chatted up a cheetah, I thought I'd like to pull a fast one.

The Swiss have an interesting army. Five hundred years without a war. Lucky for them – cos have you seen that little Swiss Army knife they have to fight with? Not much of a weapon there. Corkscrews. Bottle openers. You won't get past the first enemy soldier if he has got a spoon in his hand, let alone a bloody rifle.

Why does Sea World have a seafood restaurant?? I'm eating my fish burger and I realise - my God ... I'm eating a slow learner.

Do you know how Chicago got started? A bunch of people in New York said, 'Gee, I'm enjoying the crime and the poverty, but it just isn't cold enough. Let's go west.'

Sometimes I think war is God's way of teaching us geography.

Where lipstick is concerned, the important thing is not colour, but to accept God's final word on where your lips end.

Sign and graffiti seen in elementary school:

> # IN CASE OF FIRE
> ## Pupils must line up
> ## quietly in a single file line
> ## from smallest to tallest.

What's the logic here? Do tall people burn slower?

Every time a baseball player grabs his crotch, it makes him spit. That's why you should never date a baseball player.

I worry that the person who thought up Muzak may be thinking up something else.

Boycott shampoo!
Demand REAL poo!

Some women hold up dresses that are so ugly and they always say the same thing: 'This looks much better on.'
On what? On fire?

My grandmother, she started walking five miles a day when she was sixty.
She's ninety-seven today and we don't know where the hell she is.

The reason most people play golf is to wear clothes they would
not be caught dead in otherwise.

SCHOOLROOM DEFINITIONS

ADULT: A person who has stopped growing at both ends and is now growing in the middle.

BEAUTY PARLOUR: A place where women curl up and dye.

CANNIBAL: Someone who is fed up with people.

CHICKENS: The only animals you eat before they are born and after they are dead.

COMMITTEE: A body that keeps minutes and wastes hours.

DUST: Mud with the juice squeezed out.

EGOTIST: Someone who is usually me-deep in conversation.

GOSSIP: A person who will never tell a lie if the truth will do more damage.

HANDKERCHIEF: Cold storage.

INFLATION: Cutting money in half without damaging the paper.

MOSQUITO: An insect that makes you like flies better.

MYTH: A female moth.

RAISIN: Grape with sunburn.

SECRET: Something you tell to one person at a time.

SKELETON: A bunch of bones with the person scraped off.

TOMORROW: One of the greatest labour-saving devices of today.

TOOTHACHE: The pain that drives you to extraction.

WRINKLES: Something other people have. You have character lines.

YAWN: An honest opinion openly expressed.

If life was fair, Elvis would be alive and all the impersonators would be dead.

The truth behind Lonely Hearts ads

Women ...
Athletic – flat chested
Commitment-minded – has started choosing curtains
Communicative – you won't get a word in
Emotionally secure – on medication
Employed – has part-time job stuffing envelopes at home
Exotic beauty – would frighten a Martian
Fortyish – 49
Fun – annoying
Light drinker – lush
Loves travel – you're paying!

Non-traditional – husband still lives in the basement
Old fashioned – lights out, missionary
Open minded – desperate
Poetic – depressive schizoid
Romantic – looks better in candlelight
Rubenesque – grossly fat
Spiritual – involved in a weird cult
Stunning – egotistical
Wants soulmate – one step away from stalker
Young at heart – toothless old crone

Men ...
Athletic – watches football
Average looking – fat and bald
Distinguished looking – fat and grey
Educated – will treat you like the idiot you are
Fortyish – 55, wants 25 year old
Free spirit – will shag your sister
Friendship first – as long as it involves nudity
Good looking – arrogant bastard
Honest – pathological liar
Huggable – overweight with more body hair than Godzilla
Light drinker – heavy boozer
Likes to cuddle – can't get it up
Looks younger – if there is a bad light
Open minded – still wants to shag your sister but she is refusing
Outgoing – loud
Poetic – wrote a limerick once
Professional – owns a £30 suit bought 20 years ago at Burtons

Sensitive – closet homo
Spiritual – has been christened
Stable – stalker

Seen on the schoolyard wall:

> Our school is a good school
> It's made of bricks and plaster
> The only thing that's wrong with it
> Is the stupid fat headmaster.

> Mary had a little bear
> To which she was so kind
> And everywhere that Mary went
> She had a bear behind.

Why, when I wind up my watch, I start it; but when I wind up a project, I end it?

I didn't used to finish sentences, but now I

I've had amnesia for as long as I can remember.

*Your body is made of seventy per cent water.
So if you drink water, does that make you a cannibal?*

**Your holiday begins when your Dad says,
'I know a short cut.'**

Monica Lewinsky is now voting Republican.
She says the Democrats have left a bad taste in her mouth.

Our school is so posh we don't do vulgar fractions.

What do you call someone who's an Irish-Chinese?
Paddy Fields.

NEVER ANSWER AN ANONYMOUS LETTER.

Inland Revenue: We've got what it takes to take what you've got.

The difference between a taxidermist and the
taxman is that the taxidermist leaves the skin.

I HAD AMNESIA ONCE ... OR TWICE.

Protons have mass? I didn't even know
they were Catholic.

All I ask is a chance to prove that money can't
make me happy.

If the world was a logical place, men would ride
horses sidesaddle.

What is a 'free' gift? Aren't all gifts free?

They told me I was gullible ... and I believed them.

TWO CAN LIVE AS CHEAPLY AS ONE, FOR HALF AS LONG.

Experience is the thing you have left when
everything else is gone.

*When the only tool you have is a hammer, every
problem begins to look like a nail.*

My weight is perfect for my height ... which varies.

I used to be indecisive. Now I'm not sure.

**I went to San Francisco. I found someone's heart.
Now what?**

The cost of living hasn't affected its popularity.

It's not an optical illusion. It just looks like one.

In my day, safe sex was a padded headboard.

IF HORRIFIC MEANS TO MAKE HORRIBLE, DOES TERRIFIC MEAN TO MAKE TERRIBLE?

If people from Poland are called 'Poles', why aren't people from Holland called 'Holes'?

I remember the good old days ... when sex was safe and the motorbikes were dangerous.

I always thought a geriatric was a German footballer who scores three goals.

Why? ...

Why do they lock
petrol station toilets?
Are they afraid someone
will clean them?

Why can't you make another word using all the letters in 'anagram'?

Why don't sheep shrink when it rains?

WHY IS THE MAN WHO INVESTS ALL YOUR MONEY CALLED A BROKER?

Why do overlook and oversee mean opposite things?

Why is it that we recite at a play
and play at a recital?

Why is it that when we talk to God we're said to be praying, but when God talks to us we're schizophrenic?

Why is it that no word in the English language rhymes with month, orange, silver, or purple?

Why are a wise man and a wise guy opposites?

Why don't tomb, comb, and bomb sound alike?

WHY DO THEY PUT BRAILLE ON THE DRIVE-THROUGH BANK MACHINES?

Why isn't eleven pronounced onety one?

If the singular of GEESE is GOOSE, shouldn't a Portuguese person be called a Portugoose?

Jesus is out walking in heaven one day, the sun is shining and it is a beautiful day. He speaks pleasantries to the angels that he sees, commenting on how great it is in heaven. As he walks around a quiet corner he sees an old man sitting on a rock, head in hands, sobbing. Jesus goes to him and asks, 'Why are you crying my friend? You are in heaven. It is a wonderful place and it is such a beautiful day.'

The old man looks up at Jesus and replies, 'I am just a simple carpenter and have lost my Son. I miss him greatly.'

Jesus, trying to comfort the old man, asks him what his son was like. The old man tells him. 'Well, the thing is he is not really my son, he had nails in his hands and feet, he travelled very far and did some amazing things.'

Jesus, taking in all this information, thinks to himself, This old man is a carpenter! His son is not really his son! His son had nails in his hands! His son travelled far and did many amazing things!!!

Jesus looks the old man in the eyes and says, 'Father?'

The old man looks back and replies, 'Pinocchio??'

If someone with multiple personalities threatens to kill himself, is it considered a hostage situation?

Isn't it a bit unnerving that doctors call what they do 'practice'?

My brother plays a Pukulele – an instrument which in his hands induces vomiting.

Question time again:

Why does a giraffe have a long neck?
Because it can't stand the smell of its feet!

What do you get if you cross a hyena and a parrot?
An animal that laughs at its own jokes.

WHAT IS AN INKLING? A BABY PEN.

Why did the burglar always bathe before committing a crime?
So he would have a clean getaway.

What do you get if you cross a cow and a sheep with a goat?
The Milky Baaaa Kid.

What goes up but doesn't come down? Your age.

WHAT IS BLACK, CRAZY AND SITS ON A TREE?
A RAVEN LUNATIC.

Mum: How many millions of times have I told you not to exaggerate?

Would you believe it, today I saw a man I haven't met for thirty years?
That's nothing. Yesterday, I saw a man I've never met in all my life!

Karaoke bars combine two of the nation's greatest evils — people who shouldn't drink with people who shouldn't sing.

Neurotics build castles in the air.
Psychotics live in them
— and Psychiatrists charge them rent.

Three lessons to live by:

Lesson Number One: A crow is sitting on a tree, doing nothing all day. A small rabbit sees the crow, and asks him, 'Can I also sit like you and do nothing all day long?'
   The crow answers, 'Sure, why not.'
   So, the rabbit sits on the ground below the crow, and rests. All of a sudden, a fox appears, jumps on the rabbit and eats it.

The moral of the story is: to be sitting and doing nothing, you must be sitting very, very high up.

Lesson Number Two: A turkey is chatting with a bull. 'I would love to be able to get to the top of that tree,' sighs the turkey, 'but I haven't got the energy.'

'Well, why don't you nibble on some of my droppings?' replies the bull. 'They're packed with nutrients.'

The turkey pecks at a lump of dung and finds that it actually gives him enough strength to reach the first branch of the tree.

The next day, after eating some more dung, he reaches the second branch.

Finally after a fortnight, there he is proudly perched at the top of the tree.

He is promptly spotted by a farmer, who shoots the turkey out of the tree.

The moral of the story is: bullshit might get you to the top, but it won't keep you there.

Lesson Number Three: A little bird is flying south for the winter. It is so cold, the bird freezes and falls to the ground in a large field. While it is lying there, a cow comes by and drops some dung on it.

As the frozen bird lies there in the pile of cow dung, it begins to realise how warm it is. The dung is actually thawing him out! He lies there all warm and happy, and soon begins to sing for joy.

A passing cat hears the bird singing and comes to investigate. Following the sound, the cat discovers the bird under the pile of cow dung, and promptly digs him out and eats him!

The morals of this story are:
1) not everyone who drops shit on you is your enemy.
2) not everyone who gets you out of shit is your friend.
3) and when you're in deep shit, keep your mouth shut.

Going to church doesn't make you a Christian any more than going to McDonald's makes you a hamburger.

A coincidence is when God performs a miracle and decides to remain anonymous.

Some lessons learned:

Sometimes the majority only means that all the fools are on the same side.

I don't have to attend every argument I'm invited to.

Lead your life so you won't be ashamed to sell the family parrot to the town gossip.

Life is ten per cent what happens to you and ninety per cent how you respond to it.

Life is like an onion; you peel off one
layer at a time
and sometimes you weep.

**Learn from the mistakes of others. You can't
live long enough to make them all yourself.**

There are two things I have learned:
There is a God, and I am not Him.

*Following the path of least resistance is what
makes rivers and men crooked.*

*The people you care most about in life are taken from you too
soon, and all the less important ones just never go away.*

┌───┐

NOTICE
**Will the pupil who took the
ladder recently please return it
or further steps will be taken**
THE HEADMASTER

└───┘

Short stories:

*Two antennae meet on a roof, fall in love and get married.
The ceremony isn't much but the reception is great.*

Two cannibals are eating a clown. One says to the other: 'Does this taste funny to you?'

'Doc, I can't stop singing *The Green, Green Grass of Home*.'
   'That sounds like "Tom Jones syndrome".'
   'Is it common?'
   'It's not unusual.'

TWO COWS ARE STANDING NEXT TO EACH OTHER IN A FIELD. DAISY SAYS TO DOLLY, 'I WAS ARTIFICIALLY INSEMINATED THIS MORNING.'
   'I DON'T BELIEVE YOU,' SAYS DOLLY.
   'IT'S TRUE, NO BULL!'

Two hydrogen atoms walk into a bar. One says,
   'I've lost my electron'
      The other says, 'Are you sure?'
   The first replies, 'Yes, I'm positive . . .'

A man takes his Rottweiler to the vet and says, 'My dog's cross-eyed. Is there anything you can do for him?'
   'Well,' says the vet, 'let's have a look at him.'
   So he picks the dog up and examines his eyes, then checks his teeth. Finally, he says, 'I'm going to have to put him down.'
   'What, just because he's cross-eyed?'
   'No, because he's really heavy.'

And a longer story:

Elsie and Harry, both 91, live in a retirement home. They meet in the communal TV room and discover over time that they enjoy each other's company.

After several weeks of meeting for coffee, Harry asks Elsie out for dinner and, much to his delight, she accepts. They have a lovely evening. They dine at the most romantic restaurant in town. Despite his age, Harry is still a charmer.

Afterwards, Harry asks Elsie to join him in his room for an after-dinner drink. Things continue along a natural course and Elsie soon joins Harry for a most enjoyable roll in the hay.

As they are basking in the glow of the magic moment they'd shared, each is lost for a while in their own thoughts.

Harry is thinking: If I'd known she was a virgin, I'd have been gentler.

Elsie is thinking: If I'd known he could still do it, I'd have taken off my tights.

```
I went to buy some camouflage trousers
the other day but I couldn't find any.
```

I went to the butcher's the other day and I bet him fifty pounds that he couldn't reach the meat off the top shelf. He said, 'The steaks are too high.'

I went to a seafood disco rave last
week … and pulled a mussel.

Two Eskimos sitting in a kayak were chilly; but when they lit a fire in the craft, it sank, proving once and for all that you can't have your kayak and heat it too.

What do you call a fish with no eyes? *A fsh.*

Two fish swim into a concrete wall. One turns to the other and says, 'Dam.'

One egg for breakfast is un oeuf.

I'm desperately trying to figure out why kamikaze
pilots wear helmets.

**IF IT WEREN'T FOR ELECTRICITY WE'D ALL BE
WATCHING TELEVISION BY CANDLELIGHT.**

I am not a vegetarian because I love animals;
I am a vegetarian because I hate plants.

Our bombs are smarter than the average high school student.
At least they can find Afghanistan.

Two vampires want to go out to eat but are having a little trouble deciding where to go. They are a little tired of the local food in Transylvania and want something a little more exotic. After some discussion they decide to go to Italy because they have heard that Italian food is really good.

So, off they go to Italy and end up in Venice. On a bridge over one of the canals they hide in the shadows and wait for dinner. A few minutes later they notice a young couple walking their way. As they near, the vampires make their move. Each vampire grabs a person, sucks them dry and tosses the bodies into the canal below.

The vampires are extremely pleased with their meal and decide to have seconds. Another young couple approach a few minutes later and suffer the same fate as the first, sucked dry and then tossed into the canal below.

The vampires are now fairly full but decide to eat a dessert. In a short while a third young couple provide just that. As with the first two couples, these people are also sucked dry and tossed over the rail into the canal.

The vampires decide that they have had a marvellous dinner but that it is time to head back home and leave lovely Italy. As they start to walk away they begin to hear some singing. They are puzzled because no one else is on the bridge.

As they listen, they realise that it is coming from the canal. They look over the rail and see a big alligator in the water under the bridge, feasting on the bodies. They listen as the alligator sings ...

Wait for it ...

'Drained wops keep fallin' on my head ...'

One day little Johnny goes to his father, and asks him if he can buy him a £150 bicycle for his birthday.

Johnny's father says, 'Johnny, we have an eighty thousand pound mortgage on the house, and you want me to buy you a bicycle? Wait until Christmas.'

Christmas comes around, and Johnny asks again. The father says, 'Well, the mortgage is still extremely high, and I have had a bad year at work. Sorry, ask me again some other time.'

Two days later, the boy is seen walking out of the house with all his belongings in a suitcase. The father feels sorry for him, and asks him why he is leaving.

The boy says, 'This morning I was walking past your room, and I heard you say that you were pulling out, and mummy said that you should wait because she was coming too ... And I'll be DAMNED if I get stuck with an eighty thousand pound mortgage!'

When I was a kid I used to pray every night for a new bike. Then I realised that The Lord doesn't work that way, so I stole one and asked him to forgive me.

A teacher has forwarded this list of comments from test papers and essays allegedly submitted by elementary, junior and secondary school students:

The body consists of three parts - the branium, the borax and the abominable cavity. The branium contains the brain, the borax contains the heart and lungs and the abominable cavity contains the bowels, of which there are five a, e, i, o and u.

Nitrogen is not found in Ireland because it is not found in a free state.

H2O is hot water and CO2 is cold water.

To collect fumes of sulphur, hold a deacon over a flame in a test tube.

When you smell an odourless gas, it is probably carbon monoxide.

Water is composed of two gins, Oxygin and Hydrogin. Oxygin is pure gin. Hydrogin is gin and water.

Three kinds of blood vessels are arteries, veins and caterpillars.

Blood flows down one leg and up the other.

Respiration is composed of two acts, first inspiration and then expectoration.

The moon is a planet just like the earth, only it is even deader.

Homogenised milk comes from a gay cow.

Dew is formed on leaves when the sun shines down on them and makes them perspire.

A super saturated solution is one that holds more than it can hold.

Mushrooms always grow in damp places and so they look like umbrellas.

The pistol of a flower is its only protection against insects.

The skeleton is what is left after the insides have been taken out and the outsides have been taken off. The purpose of the skeleton is something to hitch meat to.

A permanent set of teeth consists of eight canines, eight cuspids, two molars and eight cuspidors.

The tides are a fight between the Earth and moon. All water tends towards the moon, because there is no water in the moon and nature abhors a vacuum. I forget where the sun joins in this fight.

A fossil is an extinct animal. The older it is, the more extinct it is.

Equator: A menagerie lion running around the Earth through Africa.

Germinate: To become a naturalised German.

Litter: a nest of young puppies.

Magnet: something you find crawling all over a dead cat.

Momentum: what you give a person when they are going away.

Planet: a body of earth surrounded by sky.

Rhubarb: a kind of celery gone bloodshot.

Vacuum: a large, empty space where the Pope lives.

Before giving a blood transfusion, find out if the blood is affirmative or negative.

To remove dust from the eye, pull the eye down over the nose.

For a nosebleed: put the nose much lower than the body until the heart stops.

For dog bite: put the dog away for several days. If he has not recovered, then kill it.

For head cold: use an agoniser to spray the nose until it drops in your throat.

To keep milk from turning sour: keep it in the cow.

For fainting: rub the person's chest, or, if a lady, rub her arm above the hand instead. Or put the head between the knees of the nearest medical doctor.

To prevent contraception, use a condominium.

Lysdexia is a peech imspediment I live to learn with . . .

If only women came with pull-down menus and on-line help.

Circular Definition: see Definition, Circular.

Grow your own dope - plant a politician.

The buck doesn't even slow down here!

Don't assume malice for what stupidity can explain.

If you think talk is cheap, try hiring a lawyer.

THE ONLY CURE FOR INSOMNIA IS TO GET MORE SLEEP

Advice is free; the right answer will cost plenty.

Stupidity does not qualify as a handicap: park elsewhere!

18 things we can learn from dogs

1. Never pass up the opportunity to go for a walk.
2. Allow the experience of fresh air and the wind in your face to be pure ecstasy.
3. When loved ones come home, always run to greet them.
4. When it's in your best interest, always practise obedience.
5. Let others know when they've invaded your territory.
6. Take naps and always stretch before rising.
7. Run, romp and play daily.
8. Eat with gusto and enthusiasm.
9. Be loyal.
10. Never pretend to be something you're not.
11. If what you want lies buried, dig until you find it.
12. When someone is having a bad day, be silent, sit close by and nuzzle them gently.
13. Delight in the simple joy of a long walk.
14. Thrive on attention and let people touch you.
15. Avoid biting when a simple growl will do.
16. On hot days, drink lots of water and lie under a shady tree.
17. When you are happy, dance around and wag your entire body.
18. No matter how often you are criticised, don't get a guilt complex and pout but just run right back and make friends.

REMEMBER: TEACHER IS AN ANAGRAM OF CHEATER.

These are extracts from actual letters sent to various councils and housing associations across the UK:

I want some repairs done to my cooker as it has backfired and burnt my knob off.

I wish to complain that my father hurt his ankle very badly when he put his foot in the hole in his back passage.

... And their eighteen-year-old son is continually banging his balls against my fence.

I wish to report that tiles are missing from the outside toilet roof. I think it was bad wind the other night that blew them off.

My lavatory seat is cracked; where do I stand?

I am writing on behalf of my sink that is coming away from the wall.

Will you please send someone to mend the garden path. My wife tripped and fell on it yesterday and now she is pregnant. We are getting married in September and we would like it in the garden before we move into the house.

I request permission to remove my drawers in the kitchen.

Can you please tell me when the repairs will be done as my wife is about to become an expectant mother ... Fifty per cent of the walls are damp, fifty per cent have crumbling plaster and the rest are plain filthy.

I am still having problems with smoke in my new drawers.

The toilet is blocked and we cannot bath the children until it is cleared.

Will you please send a man to look at my water; it is a funny colour and not fit to drink.

Our lavatory seat is broken in half and is now in three pieces.

Would you please send a man to repair my spout. I am an old age pensioner and need it badly.

I want to complain about the farmer across the road; every morning at five his cock wakes me up and it's now getting too much for me.

The man next door has a large erection in the back garden, which is unsightly and dangerous.

Our kitchen floor is damp. We have two children and would like a third so please send someone round to do something about it.

I am a single woman living in a downstairs flat and would you please do something about the noise made by the man I have on top of me every night.

Please send a man with the right tool to finish the job and satisfy my wife.

I have had the clerk of the works down on the kitchen floor six times but I still have no satisfaction.

This is to let you know that our lavatory seat is broken and we can't get BBC2.

My bush is really overgrown round the front and my back passage has fungus growing in it.

And he's got this huge tool that vibrates the whole house and I just can't take it anymore.

... That is his excuse for dogs' mess that I find hard to swallow.

One of the oldest forms of graffiti was the writing scrawled on the small wooden crosses which used to mark human graves. As the stone masons took over, the inscriptions became more formal – but not always more respectful!

On the grave of Ezekial Aikle in East Dalhousie cemetery, Nova Scotia:

Here lies
Ezekial Aikle
Age 102
The Good
Die Young.

In a London, England cemetery:

Ann Mann
Here lies Ann Mann,
Who lived an old maid
But died an old Mann.
Dec. 8, 1767

In an English country cemetery:

Here lies Anna Wallace
The children of Israel wanted bread
And the Lord sent them manna,
Old clerk Wallace wanted a wife,
And the Devil sent him Anna.

Playing with names in a New Mexico cemetery:

Here lies
Johnny Yeast
Pardon me
For not rising.

Touching memory of a car accident in a Pennsylvania cemetery:

Here lies the body
of Jonathan Blake
Stepped on the gas
Instead of the brake.

In a Silver City, Nevada, cemetery:

Here lays Butch,
We planted him raw.
He was quick on the trigger,
But slow on the draw.

An epitaph in a Vermont cemetery:

*Sacred to the memory of
my husband John Barnes
who died January 3, 1803
His comely young widow, aged 23, has
many qualifications of a good wife, and
yearns to be comforted.*

A lawyer's epitaph in England:

<u>Sir John Strange</u>
Here lies an honest lawyer,
And that is Strange.

Someone determined to be anonymous in Stowe, Vermont:

I was somebody.
Who, is no business
Of yours.

Lester Moore was a Wells Fargo station agent in Arizona in the 'Wild West' days of the 1880s. He is buried in the Boot Hill cemetery in Tombstone and *his* tombstone reads:

Here lies Lester Moore
Four slugs from a .44
No Les No More.

And more recently:

HERE LIES THE DENTIST RAFFERTY,
HE'S NOW FILLING HIS LAST CAVITY.

I FOUND THE TRUTH
CONTENT I LIE.

In a Georgia cemetery:

I told you I was sick!

John Penny's epitaph in the Wimborne, England, cemetery:

Reader if cash thou art
In want of any
Dig 4 feet deep
And thou wilt find a Penny.

On Margaret Daniels's grave at Hollywood cemetery, Richmond, Virginia:

She always said her feet were killing her but nobody believed her.

In a cemetery in Hertfordshire, England:

On the 22nd of June –
Jonathan Fiddle –
Went out of tune.

Anna Hopewell's grave in Enosburg Falls, Vermont has an epitaph that sounds like something from a Laurel and Hardy film:

Here lies the body of our Anna
Done to death by a banana
It wasn't the fruit that laid her low
But the skin of the thing that made her go.

More fun with names with Owen Moore in Battersea, London, England:

```
          Gone away
         Owin' more
      Than he could pay.
```

Someone in Winslow, Maine, USA didn't like a Mr Wood:

In Memory of Beza Wood departed this life
Nov. 2, 1837, Aged 45 yrs.
Here lies one Wood
Enclosed in wood
One Wood
Within another.
The outer wood
Is very good:
We cannot praise
The other.

On a grave from the 1880s in Nantucket, Massachusetts:

Under the sod and under the trees
Lies the body of Jonathan Pease.
He is not here, there's only the pod:
Pease shelled out and went to God.

The grave of Ellen Shannon in Girard, Pennsylvania is certainly consumer friendly:

Who was fatally burned
March 21, 1870
by the explosion of a lamp
filled with 'R.E. Danforth's
Non-Explosive Burning Fluid'.

In a Thurmont, Maryland, cemetery:

HERE LIES AN ATHEIST
ALL DRESSED UP
AND NO PLACE TO GO.

Harry Edsel Smith of Albany, New York:

Born 1903 – Died 1942
Looked up the elevator shaft to see if
the car was on the way down. It was.

Seen on a tombstone in a UK cemetery:

REMEMBER MAN, AS YOU WALK BY,
AS YOU ARE NOW, SO ONCE WAS I,
AS I AM NOW, SO SHALL YOU BE,
REMEMBER THIS AND FOLLOW ME.

Replying, some wag has scrawled in felt tip pen underneath:

To follow you I'll not consent,
Until I know which way you went.

He, who loses money, loses much;
He, who loses a friend, loses much more;
He, who loses faith, loses all.

Below are some amusing anecdotes and graffiti seen posted on office noticeboards:

THOUGHT FOR THE DAY

There is more money being spent on breast implants and Viagra than on Alzheimer's research.
This means that by 2030, there should be a large elderly population with perky boobs and huge erections and absolutely no recollection of what to do with them.

I don't work here. I'm a consultant.

Thank you. We're all refreshed and challenged by your unique point of view.

I'll try being nicer if you'll try being smarter.

I will always cherish the initial misconceptions I had about you.

I'm not being rude. You're just insignificant.

It sounds like English, but I can't understand a word you're saying.

I'm really easy to get along with once you people learn to worship me.

The fact that no one understands you doesn't mean you're an artist.

OK. I was wrong. You're a piss-artist.

I don't know what your problem is, but I'll bet it's hard to pronounce.

Any connection between your reality and mine is purely coincidental.

I have plenty of talent and vision. I just don't give a damn.

I'm already visualising the Sellotape over your mouth.

What am I? Flypaper for freaks!?

Yes, I am an agent of Satan, but my duties are largely ceremonial.

You sound reasonable ... Time to up the medication.

It's a thankless job, but I've got a lot of karma to burn off.

No, my powers can only be used for good.

How about never? Is never good for you?

I'm out of my mind, but feel free to leave a message ...

Who me? I just wander from room to room.

It might look like I'm doing nothing, but at the cellular level I'm really quite busy.

At least I have a positive attitude about my destructive habits.

You are validating my inherent mistrust of strangers.

I see you've set aside this special time to humiliate yourself in public.

And your insignificant, guttersnipish, blithering idiotic opinion would be ...?

Do I look like a people person?

I started out with nothing and still have most of it left.

Does your train of thought have a caboose?

Errors have been made. Others will be blamed.

Allow me to introduce my selves.

Well, for you, this day was a total waste of make-up.

A cubicle is just a padded cell without a door.

Stress is when you wake up screaming and you realise you haven't fallen asleep yet.

Nice perfume. Must you marinade in it?

Chaos, panic and disorder — my work here is done.

I thought I wanted a career. It turns out I just wanted the paycheques.

I like you. You remind me of when I was young and stupid.

Someday, we'll look back on this, laugh nervously and change the subject.

Seen on a noticeboard in a solicitors' office:

The top ten things that sound dirty in law, but aren't:

10. *Have you looked through her briefs?*
9. *He is one hard judge!*
8. *Counsel, let's do it in chambers.*
7. *His attorney withdrew at the last minute.*
6. *Is it a penal offence?*
5. *Better leave the handcuffs on.*
4. *For £200 an hour, she better be good!*
3. *Can you get him to drop his suit?*
2. *The judge gave her the stiffest one he could.*
1. *Think you can get me off?*

And, written on the wall of a Crown Court urinal:

SHOULDN'T A HUNG JURY BE ALL MALE?

On the office noticeboard:

13 things that you should learn from life

1. Never, under any circumstances, take a sleeping pill and a laxative on the same night.
2. If you had to identify, in one word, the reason why the human race has not achieved, and never will achieve, its full potential, that word would be 'meetings'.

3. There is a very fine line between 'hobby' and 'mental illness'.
4. People who want to share their religious views with you almost never want you to share yours with them.
5. You should not confuse your career with your life.
6. Never lick a steak knife.
7. The most destructive force in the universe is gossip.
8. You will never find anybody who can give you a clear and compelling reason why we put the clocks back in winter.
9. You should never say anything to a woman that even remotely suggests that you think she's pregnant unless you can see an actual baby emerging from her at that moment.
10. There comes a time when you should stop expecting other people to make a big deal about your birthday. That time is age eleven.
11. The one thing that unites all human beings, regardless of age, gender, religion, economic status or ethnic background, is that, deep down inside, we ALL believe that we are above average drivers.
12. A person who is nice to you but rude to a waiter, is not a nice person. (This is very important. It never fails.)
13. Never be afraid to try something new. Remember that a lone amateur built the Ark. A large group of professionals built the *Titanic*.

Work *v* prison:

In prison you spend the majority of your time in an 12x10 cell.
At work you spend most of your time in an 8x8 cubicle.

In prison you get three meals a day.
At work you get a break for one meal and you have to pay for it.

In prison you get time off for good behaviour.
At work you get rewarded for good behaviour with more work.

In prison you can watch TV and play games.
At work you get fired for watching TV and playing games.

In prison a guard locks, unlocks, opens and closes all doors for you.
At work you must carry around a security card and unlock and open all doors yourself.

In prison you get your own toilet.
At work you have to share.

In prison they allow visits by family and friends.
At work you can't even speak to family and friends.

In prison all expenses are paid by taxpayers, with no work required.
At work, you get to pay all the expenses to go to work and then they deduct taxes from your salary to pay for the prisoners.

In prison you spend most of your life looking through bars from the inside wanting to get out.
At work you spend most of your time wanting to get out and inside bars.

In prison you can join many programmes that you can leave at any time.
At work there are some programmes you can never get out of.

In prison there are wardens who are often sadistic and psychotic.
At work they are called managers.

SEASONAL NOTICE

Continuing the current trend of large-scale mergers and acquisitions, it was announced today at a press conference that Christmas and Chanukah will merge.

An industry source said that the deal had been in the works for about 1300 years.

While details were not available at press time, it is believed that the overhead cost of having twelve days of Christmas and eight days of Chanukah was becoming prohibitive for both sides. By combining forces, we're told, the world will be able to enjoy consistently high-quality service during the Fifteen Days of *Chrismukah*, as the new holiday is being called.

Massive layoffs are expected, with lords a-leaping and maids a-milking being the hardest hit. As part of the conditions of the agreement, the letters on the *dreydl*, currently in Hebrew, will be replaced by Latin, thus becoming unintelligible to a wider audience.

Also, instead of translating to 'A great miracle happened there', the message on the *dreydl* will be the more generic, 'Miraculous stuff happens.' In exchange, it is believed that Jews will be allowed to use Santa Claus and his vast merchandising resources for buying and delivering their gifts.

One of the sticking points holding up the agreement for at least three hundred years was the question of whether Jewish children could leave milk and a mince pie for Santa, even after having eaten meat for dinner. A breakthrough came last year, when Mr Kipling was finally declared to be kosher. All sides appeared happy about this.

A spokesman for Christmas Ltd declined to say whether a takeover of Kwanzaa might not be in the works as well. He merely pointed out that, were it not for the independent existence of Kwanzaa, the merger between Christmas and Chanukah might indeed be seen as an unfair cornering of the holiday market. Fortunately for all concerned, he said, Kwanzaa will help to maintain the competitive balance.

He then closed the press conference by leading all present in a rousing rendition of 'Oy Vey, All Ye Faithful'.

In 2002 the American oil giant Enron collapsed, causing a flurry of accusations about financial irregularities and a US investigation into the company's accounts. This led to the following appearing on a City office noticeboard:

Is this is how Enron learned Economics?

A concrete-truck driver moves to Texas and buys a donkey from an old farmer for £100. The farmer agrees to deliver the donkey the next day.

The next day, the farmer drives up and says, 'Sorry, but I have some bad news. The donkey died.'

'Well, then, just give me my money back.'

'I can't do that. I went and spent it already.'

'OK, then. Just unload the donkey.'

'What ya gonna do with him?'

'I'm going to raffle him off.'

'You can't raffle off a dead donkey!'

'Sure I can. Watch me. I just won't tell anybody he's dead.'

A month later the farmer meets up with the readi-mix driver and asks, 'What happened with that dead donkey?'

'I raffled him off. I sold five hundred tickets at two pounds apiece and I made a profit of £898.'

'Didn't anyone complain?'

'Just the guy who won. So I gave him his two quid back.'

Husband and wife

A husband and wife are getting all snuggly in bed. The passion is heating up. But then the wife stops and says, 'I don't feel like it, I just want you to hold me.'

The husband says, 'WHAT??'

The wife explains that he must be in tune with her emotional needs as a Woman.

The husband realises that nothing is going to happen tonight and he might as well deal with it.

So the next day the husband takes her shopping at a big department store. He walks around and has her try on three very expensive outfits. She can't decide which one to have.

He tells his wife to take all three of them. Then they go over and get matching shoes worth £175 each pair. And then they go to the jewellery department where she gets a set of diamond earrings. The wife is so excited. She thinks her husband has flipped out but she does not care. She goes for a tennis bracelet.

The husband says, 'You don't even play tennis but, OK, if you like it then let's get it.'

The wife is jumping up and down so excited she cannot even believe what is going on. She says, 'I am ready to go. Let's go to the cashier.'

The husband stops and says, 'No honey, I don't feel like buying all this stuff now.' The wife's face goes blank.

'No honey – I just want you to HOLD this stuff for a while.'

The look on her face is indescribable and she is about to explode – and the husband says, 'You must be in tune with my financial needs as a Man.'

Twenty thoughts for those who take life too seriously:

1. Save the whales. Collect the whole set.
2. A day without sunshine is like ... night.
3. On the other hand ... you have different fingers.
4. Ninety-nine per cent of lawyers give the rest a bad name.
5. I wonder how much deeper the ocean would be without sponges.
6. Honk if you love peace and quiet.
7. Nothing is foolproof to a talented fool.
8. He who laughs last, thinks the slowest.
9. For every action there is an equal and opposite criticism.
10. Bills travel through the mail at twice the speed of cheques.
11. No one is listening until you make a mistake.
12. The hardness of butter is directly proportional to the softness of the bread.
13. To steal ideas from one person is plagiarism; to steal from many is research.
14. Monday is an awful way to spend one-seventh of your life.
15. Two wrongs are only the beginning.
16. The sooner you fall behind the more time you'll have to catch up.
17. Change is inevitable – except from vending machines.
18. Two wrongs may not make a right; but two Wrights made an aeroplane.
19. The early bird may get the worm, but the second mouse gets the cheese.
20. Love may be blind but marriage is a real eyeopener.

20 SAYINGS OUR STAFF WOULD LIKE TO SEE ON THOSE OFFICE INSPIRATIONAL POSTERS

1. Rome did not create a great empire by having meetings . . . they did it by killing all those who opposed them.
2. If you can stay calm, while all around you is chaos . . . then you probably haven't completely understood the dire seriousness of the situation.
3. Doing a job RIGHT the first time gets the job done. Doing the job WRONG fourteen or fifteen times gives you job security.
4. Eagles may soar, but weasels don't get sucked into jet engines.
5. Artificial Intelligence is no match for Natural Stupidity.
6. A person who smiles in the face of adversity ... probably has a scapegoat.
7. Plagiarism saves time.
8. If at first you don't succeed, try management.
9. Never put off until tomorrow what you can avoid altogether.
10. TEAMWORK ... means never having to take all the blame yourself.
11. The holidays will continue until morale improves.
12. Never underestimate the power of very stupid people in large groups.
13. We waste time, so you don't have to.
14. Hang in there, retirement is only thirty years away.
15. Go the extra mile. It makes your boss look like an incompetent slacker.

16. A snooze button is a poor substitute for no alarm clock at all.
17. When the going gets tough, take a coffee break.
18. INDECISION is the key to FLEXIBILITY.
19. Succeed in spite of management.
20. Aim Low, Reach Your Goals, Avoid Disappointment.

Seen pinned on a restaurant noticeboard near to the bar:

The Dinner Party

A wife and her husband are having a dinner party for all the major business figures in Rome, Italy. The wife is very excited about this and she wants everything to be perfect. At the very last minute, she realises that she doesn't have any snails for this dinner party, so she asks her husband to run down to the beach with a bucket she handed him to gather some snails. Very grudgingly he agrees.

He takes the bucket, walks out the door, down the steps, and out to the beach. As he is collecting the snails, he notices a beautiful woman strolling alongside the water just a little further down the beach. He keeps thinking to himself, 'Wouldn't it be great if she would even just come down and talk to me.' He goes back to gathering the snails. All of a sudden he looks up, and the beautiful woman is standing right over him.

They get to talking, and she invites him back to her place. They are at her apartment a distance down the beach, and they start messing around. It gets so hot and heavy, that he is exhausted afterwards and passes out. At seven o'clock the next morning he wakes up and exclaims, 'Oh no!!! My wife's dinner party!!!' He gathers all his clothes, puts them on very fast, grabs his bucket, and runs out of the door.

He runs down the beach all the way to his apartment. He runs up the stairs of his apartment. He is in such a hurry that when he gets to the top of the stairs, he drops the bucket of snails. There are snails all down the stairs.

The door opens just then, with a very angry wife standing in the doorway wondering where he's been all this time.

He looks at the snails all down the steps, then he looks at her and then back at the snails and says: 'Come on guys, we're almost there!'

Ladies – forget home cooking and eat here – it's quicker and you can keep an eye on your husband.

Seen on a noticeboard at a computer software company:

Dodgy female software
WARNING to all computer users

I am currently running the latest version of Girlfriend 5.0 and having some problems.
I've been running the same version of Drinking Buddies 1.0 for years as my primary application, and all the Girlfriend releases have always conflicted with it.
I hear that Drinking Buddies won't crash if you minimise Girlfriend with the sound off, but since I can't find the switch to turn it off, I just run them separately and it works OK.

Girlfriend also seems to have a problem coexisting with Karaokeware.

Often trying to abort my Karaoke program with some sort of timing incompatibility.

I probably should have stayed with Girlfriend 1.0, but I thought I might see better performance with Girlfriend 2.0.

After months of conflicts, I consulted a friend who has experience with Girlfriend 2.0. He said I probably didn't have enough cache to run Girlfriend 2.0 and eventually it would require a Token Ring upgrade to run properly. He was right.

As soon as I purged my cache, Girlfriend 2.0 uninstalled itself.

Shortly after that, I installed a Girlfriend 3.0 beta. All the bugs were supposed to be gone, but the first time I used it, it gave me a virus.

After a hard drive clean up and thorough virus scan I very cautiously upgraded to Girlfriend 4.0, this time using a SCSI probe and virus protection. It worked OK for a while until I discovered Girlfriend 1.0 wasn't completely uninstalled! I tried to run Girlfriend 1.0 again with Girlfriend 4.0 still installed, but Girlfriend 4.0 has an unadvertised feature that automatically senses the presence of Girlfriend 1.0.

Both versions communicated with each other in some way, resulting in the immediate removal of both versions.

The version I have now works pretty well; but like all versions, there are still some problems. The Girlfriend package is written in some obscure language that I can't understand, much less re-programme.

And I've never liked how Girlfriend is totally 'object-oriented'.

A year ago, a friend upgraded his version to GirlfriendPlus 1.0, which is a Terminate-and-Stay resident version. He discovered GirlfriendPlus 1.0 expires within a year if you don't upgrade to Fiancee 1.0. So he did.

Soon after that, he had to upgrade to Wife 1.0, which he describes as a 'huge resource hog'. It has taken up all his space, so he can't load anything else.

One of the primary reasons that he upgraded to Wife is because it came bundled with FreeSex 1.0.

Well, it now turns out that the resource allocation module of Wife 1.0 sometimes prohibits access to FreeSex (particularly the new Plug and Play items he wanted to try).

On top of that, Wife 1.0 must be running on a well warmed-up system before he can do anything. In addition, although he did not ask for it, Wife 1.0 came with Mother-In-Law 1.0, which has an automatic popup feature he can't disable. I told him to install Mistress 1.0, but he said that he heard that if you try to run it without first uninstalling Wife, then Wife 1.0 will delete MSMoney files before uninstalling itself. Then Mistress 1.0 won't install anyway, due to insufficient resources.

A note seen pinned up in a company office in Washington DC:

Can you imagine working at this company? It has a little over 500 employees with the following statistics:

29 have been accused of spousal abuse
7 have been arrested for fraud
19 have been accused of writing bad cheques
117 have bankrupted at least two businesses
3 have been arrested for assault
71 cannot get a credit card due to bad credit
14 have been arrested on drug-related charges
8 have been arrested for shoplifting
21 are current defendants in lawsuits
In 1998 alone, 84 were stopped for drunk driving

Can you guess which organisation this is? Give up?

It's the 535 members of the United States Congress.
The same group that perpetually rolls out hundreds and hundreds of new laws designed to keep the rest of the US population in line.

Many years ago a young man was sent to prison while overseas for selling drugs. Back home in England, a friend of his scrawled the following graffiti on a Soho pub wall, right in the heart of London's theatreland:

Tim Davey got two years for selling shit.

It was not long before some wag wrote underneath:

Poor sod! Lew Grade got a knighthood for doing the same thing

A few words of advice from someone you don't know...

The main accomplishment of almost all organised protests is to annoy people who are not in them.

If there really is a God who created the entire universe with all of its glories, and He decides to deliver a message to humanity, He WILL NOT use, as His messenger, a cable TV preacher.

No matter what happens, somebody will find a way to take it too seriously.

And:

When trouble arises and things look bad, there is always one individual who perceives a solution and is willing to take command; very often, that individual is crazy.

42.7 per cent of all statistics are made up on the spot.

A conscience is what hurts when all your other parts feel so good.

Essex girl again. This time, with some of her cookbook notes:

MONDAY:
It's fun to cook for Shawn. Today I made angel food cake. The recipe said beat 12 eggs separately. The neighbours were nice enough to loan me some extra bowls.

TUESDAY:
Shawn wanted fruit salad for supper. The recipe said serve 'without dressing'. So I didn't dress. What a surprise when Shawn brought a friend home for supper.

WEDNESDAY:
A good day for rice. The recipe said wash thoroughly before steaming the rice. It seemed kind of silly but I took a bath anyway. I can't say it improved the rice any.

THURSDAY:
Today Shawn asked for salad again. I tried a new recipe. It said prepare ingredients, then toss on a bed of lettuce one hour before serving. Shawn asked me why I was rolling around in the garden.

FRIDAY:

I found an easy recipe for birthday cake. It said put the ingredients in a bowl and 'beat it'. There must have been something wrong with this recipe. When I got back, everything was the same as when I left.

SATURDAY:

Shawn did the shopping today and brought home a chicken. He asked me to dress it for Sunday (oh boy).

For some reason Shawn keeps counting to ten.

SUNDAY:

Shawn's parents came to dinner. I wanted to serve roast but all I had was a beef hamburger. Suddenly I had a brainwave. I put the hamburger in the oven and set the controls for roast. I don't know why but it still came out hamburger.

This has been a very exciting week. I am eager for tomorrow to come so I can try out a new recipe on Shawn. If I can talk Shawn into buying a bigger oven, I would like to surprise him with Chocolate Moose.

Seen pinned up in a US travel agency:

The following advisory note is for American travellers heading for France.
It has been compiled from information provided by the US State Department, the Central Intelligence Agency, the US Chamber of Commerce, the Food and Drug Administration, the Centres for Disease Control, and
some very expensive spy satellites that the French don't know about.

It is intended as a guide for American travellers only.

No guarantee of accuracy is ensured or intended.

General overview: France is a medium-sized foreign country situated in the continent of Europe. It is an important member of the world community, though not nearly as important as it thinks. It is bounded by Germany, Spain, Switzerland and some smaller nations of no particular consequence and with not very good shopping.

France is a very old country with many treasures, such as the Louvre and Euro-Disney. Among its contributions to western civilisation are champagne, Camembert cheese and the guillotine.

Although France likes to think of itself as a modern nation, air conditioning is little used and it is next to impossible to get decent Mexican food. One continuing exasperation for American visitors is that the people wilfully persist in speaking French, though many will speak English if shouted at. As in any foreign country, watch your change at all times.

The people: France has a population of 54 million people, most of whom drink and smoke a great deal, drive like lunatics, are dangerously oversexed, and have no concept of standing patiently in line. The French people are in general gloomy, temperamental, proud, arrogant, aloof, and undisciplined; and those are their good points.

Most French citizens are Roman Catholic, though you would hardly guess it from their behaviour. Many people are communists, and topless sunbathing is common.

Men sometimes have girls' names like Marie, and they kiss each other when they hand out medals.

American travellers are advised to travel in groups and to wear baseball caps and colourful trousers for easier mutual recognition.

Safety: In general, France is a safe destination, though travellers are advised that, from time to time, it is invaded by Germany. By tradition, the French surrender more or less at once and, apart from a temporary shortage of Scotch whisky and increased difficulty in getting baseball scores and stock market prices, life for the visitor generally goes on much as before.

A tunnel connecting France to Britain beneath the English Channel has been opened in recent years to make it easier for the government to flee to London.

History: France was discovered by Charlemagne in the Dark Ages. Other important historical figures are Louis XIV, the Huguenots, Joan of Arc, Jacques Cousteau and Charles de Gaulle, who was President for many years and is now an airport.

Government: The French form of government is democratic but noisy. Elections are held more or less continuously, and always result in a run-off.

For administrative purposes, the country is divided into regions, departments, districts, municipalities, cantons, communes, villages, cafes, booths and floor tiles. Parliament consists of two chambers, the Upper and Lower (though, confusingly, they are both on the ground floor), whose members are either Gaullists or communists, neither of whom is to be trusted, frankly.

Parliament's principal preoccupations are setting off atomic bombs in the South Pacific, and acting indignant when anyone complains.

According to the most current State Department intelligence, the President now is someone named Jacques. Further information is not available at this time.

Culture: The French pride themselves on their culture, though it is not easy to see why. All their songs sound the same, and they have hardly ever made a movie that you would want to watch for anything but the nude scenes. And nothing, of course, is more boring than a French novel – except, perhaps, an evening with a French family.

Cuisine: Let's face it, no matter how much garlic you put on it, a snail is just a slug with a shell on its back. Croissants, on the other hand, are excellent, though it is impossible for most Americans to pronounce this word. In general, travellers are advised to stick to cheeseburgers at leading hotels such as Sheraton and Holiday Inn.

Economy: France has a large and diversified economy, second only to Germany's in Europe, which is surprising because people hardly work at all. If they are not spending four hours dawdling over lunch, they are on strike and blocking the roads with their lorries and tractors.

France's principal exports, in order of importance to the economy, are wine, nuclear weapons, perfume, guided missiles, champagne, high-calibre weaponry, grenade launchers, landmines, tanks, attack aircraft, miscellaneous armaments and cheese.

Public holidays: France has more holidays than any other nation in the world. Among its 361 national holidays are 197 saints' days, 37 National Liberation Days, 16 Declaration of Republic Days, 54 Return of Charles de Gaulle in Triumph as if he Won the War Single-Handed Days, 18 Napoleon Sent into Exile Days, 17 Napoleon Called Back from Exile Days, and 112 France is Great and the Rest of the World is Rubbish Days. Other important holidays are National Nuclear Bomb Day (January 12), the Feast of St Brigitte Bardot Day (March 1), and National Guillotine Day (November 12).

Conclusion: France enjoys a rich history, a picturesque and varied landscape, and a temperate climate. In short, it would be a very nice country if it weren't inhabited by French people. The best thing that can be said for it is that it is not Germany.

A word of warning: The consular services of the United States government are intended solely for the promotion of the interests of American businesses such as McDonald's, Pizza Hut and the Coca-Cola Corporation. In the event that you are the victim of a crime or serious injury involving at least the loss of a limb, report to the American Embassy between the hours of 5.15 am and 5.20 am on a Tuesday or Wednesday, and a consular official who is supremely indifferent to your plight will give you a list of qualified dentists or something similarly useless.

Remember, no one ordered you to go abroad. Personally, we always take our holidays at Miami Beach, and you are advised to as well. Thank you and good luck.

I am an abstract nude painter.
I have no paint, no canvas and no nude.
I just think about it.

In light of the news of human cloning developing, I want to know – if you pushed your own naked clone off the top of a tall building, would it be:

a) murder,
b) suicide, or
c) merely making an obscene clone fall?

4

ANAGRAMS, LIMERICKS, STRANGE REPORTS AND QUIRKY HAPPENINGS

Some graffiti artists specialise in anagrams. An anagram, as you all know, is a word or phrase made by transposing or rearranging the letters of another word or phrase. Here are some quite amazing ones!:

Mother-in-law	Woman Hitler
Ossie Ardiles	Arse is soiled
Diego Maradona	O dear, I'm a gonad
David Mellor	Dildo marvel
Tony Blair PM	I'm Tory plan B
Virginia Bottomley	I'm an evil Tory bigot
Michael Heseltine	Elect him, he's alien
Dame Agatha Christie	I am a right death case
Motorway service station	I eat coronary vomit stews
The Metropolitan Police force	I'm fellatio, the erect porno cop
Benson and Hedges	NHS been a godsend
Selina Scott	Elastic snot
Mel Gibson	Big melons
Gloria Estefan	Large fat noise

Chris Rea	Rich arse
Martina Navratilova	Variant rival to a man
Gabriela Sabatini	Insatiable airbag
Irritable Bowel Syndrome	O my terrible drains below
Evangelist	Evil's agent
Desperation	A rope ends it
The Morse Code	Here come dots
Semolina	Is no meal
A decimal point	I'm a dot in place
Eleven plus two	Twelve plus one

Someone out there either has far too much time to waste or is deadly at Scrabble, as these further examples show:

Dormitory	Dirty room
Slot machines	Cash lost in 'em
Animosity	Is no amity
Snooze alarms	Alas! No more Zs
The earthquakes	That queer shake

Of Neil Armstrong's famous quote, on landing on the moon: 'That's one small step for a man, one giant leap for mankind', the anagram is:

A thin man ran; makes a large stride, left planet, pins flag on moon! On to Mars!

Even Shakespeare is not immune from the anagram treatment. 'To be or not to be, that is the question. Whether tis nobler in the mind to suffer the slings and arrows of outrageous fortune' translates as:

In one of the Bard's best-thought-of tragedies, our insistent hero, Hamlet, queries on two fronts about how life turns rotten.

And for the finale here: PRESIDENT CLINTON OF THE USA can be rearranged ... with no letters left over . . . using each letter only once . . . into:

TO COPULATE HE FINDS INTERNS

Here is a copy of a note pinned up in an office. The words are all taken from the dictionary, altered by adding, subtracting or changing just one letter, and now supplied with a new definition:

Reintarnation: *Coming back to life as a hillbilly.*
Foreploy: *Any misrepresentation about yourself for the purpose of obtaining sex.*
Giraffiti: *Vandalism sprayed very, very high.*
Tatyr: *A lecherous Mr Potato Head.*
Sarchasm: *The gulf between the author of sarcastic wit and the recipient who doesn't get it.*
Inoculatte: *To take coffee intravenously when you are running late.*
Hipatitis: *Terminal coolness.*
Osteopornosis: *A degenerate disease.*
Burglesque: *A poorly planned break-in. (See: Watergate)*
Karmageddon: *It's like, when everybody is sending off all these really bad vibes, right? And then the Earth explodes.*
Glibido: *All talk and no action.*
Dopeler effect: *The tendency of stupid ideas to seem smarter when they come at you rapidly.*

Intaxication: *Euphoria at getting a refund from the Inland Revenue, which lasts until you realise it was your money to start with.*
Ignoranus: *A person who's both stupid and an arsehole.*

One of the most popular graffiti forms is the limerick. It is easy to see why. Trying to compose an unusual rhyming couplet is a challenge that most people have tried at some time or other. Here are some that have graced walls as anonymous graffiti:

There once was a Man named McSweeney,
Who spilled some gin on his weenie,
Just to be couth,
He added vermouth,
And slipped his chick a Martini!

There was a young man from Cape Horn,
Who wished he had never been born,
And he wouldn't have been,
If his father had seen,
That the tip of the rubber was torn!

The limerick form is complex,
Its contents run chiefly to sex,
It burgeons with virgins,
And masculine urge-ons,
And swarms with erotic effects.

There once was a man from Peru,
Who dreamed of eating his shoe,
He awoke with a fright,
In the middle of the night,
And found that his dream had come true!

There once was a lady, Ilene,
Who lived on distilled kerosene,
But she started absorbin',
A new hydrocarbon,
And since then she'd never benzene.

There once was a lady from Hyde,
Who ate a green apple and died,
While her lover lamented,
The apple fermented,
And made cider inside her inside.

There was a lady who triplets begat,
Matt, Pat and Tat.
It was great fun breeding,
But real trouble feeding,
'Cause she didn't have a tit for Tat.

On Hallowe'en a young girl from the coast,
Was screwed in the park by a ghost.
At the height of orgasm,
This pale ectoplasm,
Cried, 'I think I can feel it – almost.'

'MY NIECES ARE DARLINGS,' SAID SID,
'TO OBLIGE THEM I DO AS I'M BID.'
AS HE TUCKED THEM IN BED,
HE ASKED, 'WHAT'S TO BE READ?'
'UNCLE RHEMUS,' THEY CRIED, AND HE DID.

There once was a young girl from Norway,
Who hung by her feet from the doorway.
This worked out quite well,
'Cause when you rang her bell,
It actually turned out to be foreplay!

There once was a poet named Dan,
Whose poetry never would scan.
When told this was so,
He said, 'Yes, I know,
It's because I try to put every possible syllable into the very
last line that I can.'

There was a young lady named Myrtle,
Who amused herself with a sea-turtle.
And what was phenomenal,
A swelling abdominal,
Revealed that the turtle . . . was fertile!

I once met a beautiful Persian,
A shy one who needed coercion.
So I gave her a smile,
And she thought for a while,
Then allowed me to make an insertion.

A young engineer named Paul,
Was equipped with an octagonal ball.
The square of his weight,
Times his penis, plus eight,
Is his phone number, give him a call.

THERE WAS A YOUNG LADY FROM BUDE,
WHO HAD SCENES OF OLD ENGLAND TATTOOED.
HER BOYFRIEND, ONE DAY,
WENT THE WHOLE PENNINE WAY,
WITH CHEDDAR GORGE STILL TO BE VIEWED.

A gay who lived in Khartoum,
Took a lesbian up to his room,
And they argued all night,
Over who had the right,
To do what, and with which, and to whom.

A lovely young lady at sea,
Complained that it hurt her to pee.
Said the burly First Mate,
'That accounts for the fate
of the Cook and the Captain and me.'

There once was a rooster from Tarmer,
Who thought he was quite the charmer,
Until, by the shed,
He lost his proud head,
To the old rusty axe of the farmer.

There was a fat woman named Maya,
Whose belly had layer after layer.
Her gut was so huge,
She'd never seen her shoes,
And so she let the borough surveyor.

There was a young lady from Wantage,
With whom a young man took advantage.
'You'd better pay her,'
Said the Borough Surveyor,
'Because you've altered the shape of her frontage.'

There was a young man from Calcutta,
Who peeked through a hole in a shutter.
All he could see,
Was a prostitute's knee,
And the bum of the chap who was up her!

A remarkable race are the Persians,
With so many sexual diversions,
They make love all day,
In the regular way,
And save up the night for perversions.

There was a young man from Taiwan,
Who ordered one ton of wonton.
His perversion proved heinous,
For he whipped out his penis,
And tied one Taiwan wonton on!

The labels on bras of old brides,
Are warnings that hang from the sides:
'This carries large boulders,
Supported by shoulders,
Removing could cause some rock slides!'

There was a poor girl on the street,
In dustbins found leftovers to eat.
She thought she had garbage stew,
That tasted like a horse's doo,
Yet insisted it tasted quite sweet.

There was a young woman named Bright,
Whose speed was much faster than light.
She set out one day,
In a relative way,
And returned on the previous night.

When an old man fell asleep in the sun,
The zipper on his fly came undone.
He awoke with a smile,
Said, 'My gosh, a sundial,
And it's nearly a quarter past one.'

There once was a lady from Exeter,
And the men in the street craned their necks at her.
One day to be rude,
She reclined in the nude,
While her parrot, a pervert, took pecks at her.

There once was a president named Bill,
Who often had quite a thrill,
As an intern named Monica,
Played like a harmonica,
All over his Capitol Hill.

There was once a man named Penn,
Who said, 'Let us do it again,
And again and again,
And again and again,
and again and again and again!'

I knew a young lady named Claire,
Who possessed a magnificent pair.
Or that's what I thought,
Till I saw one get caught,
On a thorn and begin losing air.

There once was a fellow named Ernie,
Whose profession was pushing a gurney.
From hospital room,
To the morgue and its gloom,
Was this Ernie's favorite journey.

There was a chicken farmer from Hay,
Who found his hens wouldn't lay;
The trouble was Brewster,
His champion rooster;
You see, Brewster the rooster was gay!

The latest word from the Dean,
Regarding the teaching machine,
Is that Oedipus Rex,
Could have learned about sex,
Alone without bothering the queen.

There once was a lady named Mabel,
Whose ass was as big as a table.
'Never you mind,'
Said a dear friend of mine.
'She's ready, willing, and able.'

There once was a knight named Sir Lancelot,
Whom the people all looked at askance a lot.
For whenever he'd pass,
A delectable lass,
The front of his pants would advance a lot.

I never read a limerick with 'orgy' in.
It seems they have trouble beginnin'.
On the other hand my rhymes,
At least some of the times,
Have a lot of fun and sin in!

There was a young whore from Kilkenny,
Who charged two f**** for a penny,
For half of that sum,
You could bugger her bum,
An economy practised by many.

A LIGHTHOUSE KEEPER CALLED CRIGHTON
TOOK TO SEEING A LADY FROM BRIGHTON.
BUT SHIPS RAN AGROUND,
AND SAILORS WERE DROWNED,
AS SHE WOULDN'T HAVE SEX WITH THE LIGHT ON.

There once was a lady from France,
Who kept a baboon in her pants.
Half the people who saw,
Couldn't help but guffaw,
But the rest of them asked her to dance.

There once was a man from Far Rockaway,
Who could smell a piece-of-ass about a block away.
One night he got a whiff,
But she had the 'syph',
And now it's eating his cock-a-way.

A flea and a fly in a flue,
Were imprisoned, so what could they do?
Said the fly, 'Let us flee!'
'Let us fly!' said the flea.
So they flew through a flaw in the flue.

An epicure dining at Crewe,
Found a very large bug in his stew.
Said the waiter, 'Don't shout,
And wave it about,
Or the rest will be wanting one too.'

There once was a man from Great Britain,
Who interrupted two girls at their knittin'.
Said he with a sigh,
'That park bench, well I,
Just painted it right where you're sittin'.'

THERE WAS A YOUNG HUNTER NAMED SHEPHERD,
WHO WAS EATEN FOR LUNCH BY A LEOPARD.
SAID THE LEOPARD, 'EGAD!
YOU'D BE TASTIER, LAD,
IF YOU HAD BEEN SALTED AND PEPPERED!'

There was a farmer from Leeds,
Who ate six packets of seeds.
It soon came to pass,
He was covered with grass,
And he couldn't sit down for the weeds.

Busty Sue was thrilled to bits,
To be staying at the London Ritz.
As the clerk checked her in,
He gave her a sly grin,
As he surreptitiously checked out her tits.

THERE WAS A YOUNG GIRL FROM CAPE COD,
WHO THOUGHT THAT BABIES CAME FROM GOD.
T'WASN'T THE ALMIGHTY,
WHO LIFTED HER NIGHTIE,
BUT ROGER THE LODGER, THE SOD!

A HOLLYWOOD ACTRESS OF NOTE,
BOUGHT AN EXPENSIVE FUR COAT.
THEY SAID IT WAS MINK,
BUT IT WASN'T, I THINK,
FROM THE SMELL IT WAS ANGORA GOAT.

There once was a fellow called Hough,
His mother's obscenely rough.
She's not very choosy,
Some say she's a floozy,
And not a nice sight in the buff.

There once was a girl from Illinois,
Who liked to climb trees with the boys.
Tho' she didn't flirt,
They'd look up her skirt,
With holes in their pockets for toys.

A true story pinned on a bank noticeboard, from San Francisco, USA:

A man, wanting to rob a downtown Bank of America, walks into the branch and writes: 'This iz a stikk up. Put all your muny in this bag.'

While standing in line, waiting to give his note to the teller, he begins to worry that someone has seen him write the note and might call the police before he reaches the teller window.

He therefore leaves the Bank of America and crosses the street to Wells Fargo. After waiting a few minutes in line, he hands his note to the Wells Fargo teller. She reads it and, surmising from his spelling errors that he isn't very bright, tells him that she cannot accept his stick-up note because it is written on a Bank of America deposit slip and that he will either have to fill out a Wells Fargo deposit slip or go back to Bank of America.

Looking somewhat defeated, the man says, 'OK' and leaves.

The Wells Fargo teller then calls the police who arrest the man a few minutes later, as he is waiting in line back at the Bank of America.

And:

A man walks into a corner shop with a shotgun and demands all the cash from the cash drawer. After the cashier puts the cash in a bag, the robber sees a bottle of scotch that he wants behind the counter on the shelf. He tells the cashier to put it in the bag as well, but she refuses and says, 'I don't believe you are over eighteen.'

The robber says he is, but the assistant still refuses to give it to him because she doesn't believe him. At this point the robber takes his driving licence out of his wallet and gives it to the cashier. She looks it over, agrees that the man is in fact over eighteen, and hands him the scotch, which he puts in the bag.

The robber then runs from the store with his loot. The cashier promptly calls the police and gives the name and address of the robber that she got off the licence. They arrest the robber two hours later.

A South African hospital to avoid – Pelonomi Hospital:

Date: 26 July 1996

'For several months, our nurses have been baffled to find a dead patient in the same bed every Friday morning,' a spokeswoman for the Pelonomi Hospital (Free State, South Africa) told reporters.

'There was no apparent cause for any of the deaths, and extensive checks on the air conditioning system, and a search for possible bacterial infection, failed to reveal any clues.

'However, further enquiries have now revealed the cause of these deaths. It seems that every Friday morning a cleaner would enter the ward, remove the plug that powered the patient's life support system, plug her floor polisher into the vacant socket, then go about her business. When she had finished her chores, she would plug the life support machine back in and leave, unaware that the patient was now dead. She could not, after all, hear the screams and eventual death rattle over the whirring of her polisher.

'We are sorry, and have sent a strong letter to the cleaner in question. Further, the Free State Health and Welfare Department is arranging for an electrician to fit an extra socket, so there should be no repetition of this incident.

'The enquiry is now closed.'

(From *Cape Times*. The headline of the newspaper story was, 'Cleaner Polishes Off Patients'.)

Here's one nearer to home, from a local UK newspaper:

'I have promised to keep his identity confidential,' said Jane Setherton, a spokeswoman for the Marriott Hotel, Bristol, 'but I can confirm that he is no longer in our employment. We asked him to clean one lift, and he spent four days on the job.

'When I asked him why, he replied, "Well, there are twelve of them, one on each floor, and sometimes some of them aren't there."

'Eventually we realised that he thought each floor had a different lift, and he'd cleaned the same one twelve times. We had to let him go. It seemed best all round. I understand he is now working for Woolworths.'

From a South African newspaper:

'The situation is absolutely under control,' Transport Minister Ephraem Magagula told the Swaziland parliament in Mbabane. 'Our nation's merchant navy is perfectly safe. We just don't know where it is, that's all.'

Replying to an MP's question, Minister Magagula admitted that the landlocked country had completely lost track of its only ship, the *Swazimar*. 'We believe it is in a sea somewhere. At one time, we sent a team of men to look for it, but there was a problem with drink and they failed to find it, and so, technically, yes, we've lost it a bit. But I categorically reject all suggestions of incompetence on the part of this government. The *Swazimar* is a big ship painted in the sort of nice bright colours you can see at night. Mark my words, it will turn up. The right honourable gentleman opposite is a very naughty man, and he will laugh on the other side of his face when my ship comes in.'

And from a West African newspaper:

'What is all the fuss about?' A Mr Sambu asked a hastily convened news conference at Jomo Kenyatta International Airport. 'A technical hitch like this could have happened anywhere in the world. You people are not patriots. You just want to cause trouble.'

Mr Sambu, a spokesman for an African airline, was speaking after the cancellation of a through flight from Kisumu, via Jomo Kenyatta, to Berlin: 'The forty-two passengers had boarded the plane ready for take-off, when the pilot noticed one of the tyres was flat. The airline did not possess a spare tyre, and unfortunately the airport nitrogen canister was empty. A passenger suggested taking the tyre to a petrol station for inflation, but unluckily the jack had gone missing so we couldn't get the wheel off. Our engineers tried heroically to reinflate the tyre with a bicycle pump, but had no luck, and the pilot even blew into the valve with his mouth, but he passed out.

'When I announced that the flight had to be abandoned, one of the passengers, Mr Mutu, suddenly struck me about the face with a life-jacket whistle and said we were a national disgrace. I told him he was being ridiculous, and that there was to be another flight in a fortnight. And in the meantime he would be able to enjoy the scenery around Kisumu, albeit at his own expense.'

The 2005 There's Nowt as Queer or as Stupid as Folk Awards have been released!:

RUNNER-UP No 5 From England: a motorist was unknowingly caught in an automated speed trap by a camera that photographed his car. He later received in the post a ticket for £60. Initially denying liability, he was sent a photo of his car with the speed printed thereon.

Instead of payment, he sent the police department a photograph of £60.

In response, he then received a letter from the police that contained another picture – of handcuffs.

The motorist then promptly sent the money for the fine.

RUNNER-UP No 4 Drug possession defendant Christopher Jansen: on trial in March in Michigan, USA, Christopher said he had been searched without a warrant. The prosecutor said the officer didn't need a warrant because a 'bulge' in Christopher's jacket could have been a gun.

'Nonsense,' said Christopher who happened to be wearing the same jacket that day in court. He handed it over so the judge could see it. The judge discovered a packet of cocaine in the pocket and laughed so hard he required a five minute recess to compose himself.

RUNNER-UP No 3 Oklahoma City, USA: Dennis Newton was on trial in district court for the armed robbery of a convenience store when he fired his lawyer. Assistant district attorney Larry Jones said Newton, 47, was doing a fair job of defending himself until the store manager testified that Newton was the robber.

Newton jumped up, accused the woman of lying and then said, 'I should have blown your darn head off.' The defendant paused, then quickly added, 'If I'd been the one that was there.'

The jury took 20 minutes to convict Newton and recommended a 30-year sentence.

RUNNER-UP No 2 Detroit, USA: a Mr Gattlan walked up to two patrol officers who were showing their squad car computer felon-location equipment to children in a Detroit neighbourhood. When he asked how the system worked, the officer asked him for identification. Gattlan gave them his driving licence, they entered it into the computer, and moments later they arrested him because information on the screen showed Gattlan was wanted for a two-year-old armed robbery in St Louis, Missouri.

RUNNER-UP No 1 Another from Detroit: a pair of Michigan robbers entered a record shop nervously waving revolvers. The first one shouted, 'Nobody move!' When his partner moved, the startled first bandit shot him.

THE WINNER: a North Carolina man, having purchased a case of very rare, very expensive cigars, insured them against fire (among other things). Within a month, having smoked his entire stockpile of cigars and without even having made his first premium payment on the policy, the man filed a claim against the insurance company. In his claim, the man stated the cigars were lost 'in a series of small fires'.

The insurance company refused to pay, citing the obvious reason that the man had consumed the cigars in the normal fashion.

The man sued and won. In delivering the ruling the judge, agreeing that the claim was frivolous, stated nevertheless that the man held a policy from the company in which it had warranted that the cigars were insurable and also guaranteed that it would insure against fire, without defining what it considered to be 'unacceptable fire', and was obligated to pay the claim.

Rather than endure a lengthy and costly appeal process the insurance company accepted the ruling and paid the man $15,000 for the rare cigars he lost in 'the fires'.

After the man cashed the cheque, the company had him arrested on 24 counts of arson. With his own insurance claim and using his testimony against him, the man was convicted of intentionally burning his insured property and sentenced to 24 months in jail and a $24,000 fine . . . it could only happen in America!

An employee for an Australian air company who happened to have the last name of GAY, got on a plane recently using one of his company's 'Free Flight' programmes. However, when Mr Gay tried to take his seat, he found it being occupied by a paying passenger. So, not to make a fuss, he simply chose another seat.

Unknown to Mr Gay, another of the company's flights experienced mechanical problems. The passengers of this other flight were being rerouted to various aeroplanes. A few were put on Mr Gay's flight and anyone who was holding a free 'ticket was being 'bumped'.

Company officials, armed with a list of these 'freebee' ticket holders, boarded the plane to remove the free ticket holders. Of course, our Mr Gay was not sitting in his assigned seat, so when the ticket agent approached the seat where Mr Gay was supposed to be sitting, she asked a startled customer, 'Are you Gay?'

The man shyly nodded that he was, at which point she demanded: 'Then you have to get off the plane.'

Mr Gay, overhearing what the ticket agent had said, tried to clear up the situation: 'You've got the wrong man. I'm Gay!' This caused an angry third passenger to yell, 'Hell, I'm gay too! They can't kick us all off!'

Confusion reigned as more and more passengers began yelling that the flight company had no right to remove gays from their flights. So far they have refused to comment on the incident.

Things you don't want to hear during surgery

Better save that. We'll need it for the autopsy.
Someone call the caretaker - we're going to need a mop and bucket.
Wait a minute, if this is his spleen, then what's that?
Hand me that ... uh ... that uh ... thingymebob.
Oops! Oh dear. Has anyone ever survived 500ml of this stuff before?
Blast it, the ventilator has packed up again ...
Did you know, there's big money in kidneys and this character's got two of 'em.
Everybody stand back! I lost my contact lens!
Could you stop that thing from beating? It's throwing my concentration off!
What's this doing here?

I wish I hadn't forgotten my glasses today.

Well, gentlemen, this will be an experiment for all of us.

Sterile? Well the bloody floor's clean, right?

Anyone see where I left that scalpel?

OK, now take a picture from this angle. This is truly a freak of nature.

Nurse, did this patient sign the organ donation card?

Don't worry. I think it is probably sharp enough.

She's gonna blow! Everyone take cover!!!

Sod it! Page 47 of the manual is missing!

What rotten weather it was coming here. You know I envy him, cos at least he won't be going back home in it.

FIRE! FIRE! Abandon the operation. Everyone make their own way out.

5

OFF THE WALL
INSULTING GRAFFITI AND ABUSE

One of the downsides of any public bar is the likelihood of becoming involved in an argument with someone who has had too much to drink. The upside is listening to others arguing and enjoying the insults flying through the air!

Here are some of the best verbal gems overheard in and around the public bar, together with some added public house graffiti insults:

'I PRESUME YOUR GIRLFRIEND WILL NAME HER BABY AFTER THE FATHER – ARMY!'

And, perhaps, of the same girl:

`'She's been boarded more times than the Orient Express.'`

'John Prescott is doing the best he can. There, that's scared you.'

'The only curve on my wife's body is her Adam's apple.'

'He's so smarmy, he doesn't have his hair cut, he goes for an oil change.'

'You know that organisation that freezes bodies – well, you look like a founder member.'

'My wife has the body of a twenty-year-old ... a twenty-year-old Skoda.'

'I don't know how old you are but I bet when you were young the Dead Sea was still alive!'

'You're so short, when you sit you're taller.'

And again on a shortie:

'When it rains you're the last to know.'

At a church cafeteria:

'This café is the only place where you say grace over grease.'

'He is so thick he thinks that "Vat 69" is the Pope's phone number.'

'I BET SHE CLOSES HER EYES WHEN HER HUSBAND MAKES LOVE – SHE DOESN'T WANT TO SEE HIM HAVING A GOOD TIME.'

'If she's "pushing thirty-five" it must be pleated.'

'The way your wife finds fault, you'd think there was a reward.'

'She doesn't have an enemy in the world. She's outlived them.'

'He has the manners of a gentleman – I knew they couldn't belong to him.'

'My wife has the looks that turn heads ... and stomachs too.'

'In her house the antique furniture is just stuff from her first marriage.'

'You have a great voice . . . unfortunately it's in someone else's throat.'

'He's so unlucky he probably gets paper cuts from get-well cards.'

'YOU SHOULD LEAVE AND LET LIVE.'

'My wife's way of being right is to be wrong at the top of her voice.'

'He is so thin, the crease in his trousers is him.'

'She is so ugly, her make-up comes in a snake-bite kit.'

'My wife has a new form of exercise – aerobic nagging.'

'She has a lot of class – steerage.'

'My wife speaks at 120 words a minute – with gusts up to 150.'

'My wife loves looking in the mirror admiring her looks. It's not vanity. She's just got a vivid imagination.'

'When he was a sailor he sailed across the Atlantic both ways without even taking a bath. I suppose you could say he's a genuine dirty double crosser.'

MOTHER IN LAW
'My wife asked what it would take to make her look good. I said, "About a mile."'

'WHISPER THOSE THREE LITTLE WORDS THAT WOULD MAKE HER DAY – "GO TO HELL!"'

You can always spot my wife at a party – look for two people talking. If one looks bored, then the other is my wife.'

'He's so ugly the doctor slapped his mother when he was born.'

'I wouldn't mind going out with someone who's smart, funny, and attractive. Now, if I could only find someone who is.'

(When asked out by a berk.) 'I'll give you this number. If I don't answer, that's because it's not my number.'

'IF I HAD A FACE LIKE YOURS, I WOULD TRY TO KEEP MY PANTS ON!'

'She's had more pricks than a second-hand dart board'

'Your father is so dumb he can't even pass a blood test!'

'**Your mother is so ugly she stuck her head out the window and got arrested for mooning.**'

'He's so slow he has to speed up to stop.'

' If my dog had a face like yours, I'd shave his arse and make him walk backwards!'

'Shouldn't you be somewhere downloading porn off the internet?'

'I've found stuff on the bottom of my shoe smarter than you.'

(Someone approaches you.) 'Sorry, I don't donate money to the special Olympics.'

'The most interesting part of life is death, so why can't you be interesting?'

'If only I had the time to care. But I'm very busy.'

'You're so dumb mind readers charge you half price!'

'Stop global warming ... shut your mouth!'

**'IF BRAINS WERE DYNAMITE, YOU COULDN'T BLOW
YOUR NOSE.'**

'Here's fifty pence. Go buy yourself a life.'

'You're depriving some poor village of their idiot.'

**'You're so dumb, you waited for a stop
sign to say go.'**

'When I grow up I want to be just like you. But I don't think I can become that stupid that fast.'

'Your wife's so fat, she needs a boomerang to put her belt on.'

'Your mother's so hairy, you almost died of rugburn at birth.'

'Your wife's teeth are so yellow, traffic slows down when she smiles.'

'Your girlfriend's so fat, when you get on top of her to have sex your ears pop.'

(While talking to a girl.) 'Has anybody ever mistaken you for a female?'

'You're so ugly, you walked into a haunted house and came back out with a job application.'

'You're about as much use as a condom machine in the Vatican.'

'YOUR SECRETARY IS SO FAT, WHEN HER BEEPER GOES OFF PEOPLE THINK SHE'S REVERSING!'

'You could play a few games of "connect the dots" on your face.'

'You're so stupid, I bet you couldn't count your balls and come up with the same answer twice!'

'How do you piss without getting soaked?'

'You were so ugly as a child your mum had to tie a steak around your neck so the dog would play with you.'

'Your teeth are so yellow, I can't believe it's not butter!'

'SOME WOMEN HAVE FACES THAT CAN STOP A CLOCK. SHE COULD STOP SWITZERLAND.'

'My husband never drinks unless he's alone or with someone.'

'He was descended from a long line his mother fell for.'

'He was an unwanted child. When they gave him a rattle it was still attached to the snake.'

'He's a born-again cretin.'

'HE DRINKS SO MUCH, WHEN HE SWEATS HE'S A FIRE HAZARD.'

'He's nobody's fool. He freelances.'

'Some people say she's a pain in the back. Others have a lower opinion of her.'

'He's so rich, when he catches a plane he has to check in his wallet.'

'I find her breath offensive – it's keeping her alive.'

'He's good at everything he does – and as far as I can see he usually does nothing.'

'I won't say he's a drunk but if Dracula bit him in the neck,
he'd get a Bloody Mary.'

'He has an answer for everything - the wrong one.'

'He's a boon to the whole area - a baboon.'

'People like that don't grow on trees you know –
they normally swing under them.'

'Did you hear that he was buried face down?
So he could see where he was going.'

'His death won't be listed under *Obituaries*. More
like *Neighbourhood improvements*.'

'I hear she is a business woman – her nose is
always in other people's business.'

**'THEY DO SAY HE'S VERY COURTEOUS - HE APOLOGISES
AFTER HE'S KICKED YOU.'**

'Listening to you is a perfect cure for an inferiority complex.'

'She made her money the old-fashioned way. She inherited it.'

'He's got about as many friends as an alarm clock.'

'She has a 38 inch bust – and an IQ to match.'

'He has every attribute of a dog – except loyalty.'

'The IRA have told their men to equip themselves for germ warfare – so their supporters have all bought themselves septic tanks.'

'Brains aren't everything. In your case, they're nothing.'

'Didn't I get a restraining order against you?'

'WHO LET THE DOGS OUT?'

'You are one of those people that shouldn't ask people out. You might get arrested.'

'I would go out with you, but I can't accept you for the retard you are.'

'GO OUT WITH YOU? I'D RATHER SCRAPE MY GUMS.'

'You make me want to stay a virgin.'

'Don't you ever get tired of having yourself around?'

'Don't worry. There is a good reason for you to have that stupid look on your face. You *are* stupid.'

'Well, I'd like to leave a thought with you — but where would you put it?'

'You know, you are so dull, you can't even entertain a doubt.'

'I have nothing but confidence in you – and not a lot of that.'

'You obviously have a lot of time on your hands and the wrinkles to prove it.'

'SHE'S NOT PUSHING FORTY – SHE'S DRAGGING IT.'

He has no equals – only superiors.'

'I am sure you also use your head – mostly for a rock garden.'

'You're obviously not yourself today. Enjoy it whilst you can.'

'If I had a lower IQ, I'm sure I'd enjoy your company.'

On telling an old joke, a man in the bar shouted at the raconteur:
'That joke was your father's.'
The raconteur shot back:
'And you were your mother's.'

'You should have your ears cleaned out ... with a 12-bore shotgun.'

'I am sure you're kind to your inferiors ... but where do you find them?'

'You're as useful as a one-legged man trying to put out a grass fire.'

'If you were alive you'd be a very sick man.'

'I'd make you eat those words if you had teeth.'

'SOMEONE GET A PLUMBER – THERE'S A BIG DRIP IN HERE.'

'I can see you started at the bottom ... and sank.'

'I wish my future was as bright as your suit. There's enough grease on your clothes to fry a pan of chips, you scruffy bastard.'

'Your mouth is big enough to sing duets.'

'I've seen better arguments in a bowl of alphabet soup.'

'I may not agree with what you say but I'll defend to the death your right to shut up.'

'His men would follow him anywhere ... but only out of morbid curiosity.'

And, heard around the office:

'I would not allow this employee to breed.'

'This employee is really not so much of a "has-been", but more of a definite "won't be".'

'When she opens her mouth, it seems that it is only to change feet.'

'He would be out of his depth in a roadside puddle.'

'This young lady has delusions of adequacy.'

'He sets low personal standards and then consistently fails to achieve them.'

'This employee should go far ... and the sooner he starts, the better.'

'He's got a full six-pack, but lacks the plastic thing to hold it all together.'

'She's a gross ignoramus - 144 times worse than an ordinary ignoramus.'

'He certainly takes a long time to make his pointless.'

'He doesn't have ulcers, but he's a carrier.'

'I would like to go hunting with him sometime.'

'He's been working with glue too much.'

'She would argue with a signpost.'

'He has a knack for making strangers immediately.'

'He brings a lot of joy whenever he leaves the room.'

'When his IQ reaches 50, he should sell.'

'He has a photographic memory but with the lens cover glued on.'

'A PRIME CANDIDATE FOR NATURAL DE-SELECTION.'

'I think he donated his brain to science before he was finished using it.'

'She has two brains: one is lost and the other is out looking for it.'

'If he was any more stupid, he'd have to be watered twice a week.'

'If you gave him a penny for his thoughts, you'd get change.'

'If you stand close enough to him, you can hear the ocean.'

'It's hard to believe that he beat one million other sperm to the egg.'

'One neuron short of a synapse.'

'Some drink from the fountain of knowledge ... he only gargled.'

'It takes him two hours to watch *Sixty Minutes*.'

'You're the sort who gives idiots a bad name.'

'Did I see you at the Nuremberg trials?'

'If they put a price on your head – take it.'

'Why don't you freeze your teeth and give your tongue a sleigh ride?'

'The stork that brought you should have been fined for smuggling dope.'

'My mother-in-law is 76 years of age and she doesn't use glasses. She drinks straight out of the bottle.'

'The gentleman is obviously well past his yell-by date.'

'I can see with you ignorance is a religion.'

'After meeting you, I've decided I am in favour of abortion in cases of incest.'

'All that you are you owe to your parents. Why don't you send them a penny and square the account?'

'Any similarity between you and a human is purely coincidental.'

'Anyone who told you to be yourself couldn't have given you worse advice.'

'ARE YOU ALWAYS SO STUPID OR IS TODAY A SPECIAL OCCASION?'

'As an outsider, what do you think of the human race?'

'Better at sex than anyone; now all he needs is a partner.'

'Calling you stupid would be an insult to stupid people.'

'DID YOUR PARENTS EVER ASK YOU TO RUN AWAY FROM HOME?'

'Do you ever wonder what life would be like if you'd had enough oxygen at birth?'

'Do you want people to accept you as you are or do you want them to like you?'

'Don't feel bad. A lot of people have no talent!'

'Don't let your mind wander – it's too little to be let out alone.'

'Don't thank me for insulting you. It was my pleasure.'

'Don't think; it may sprain your brain.'

'Don't you have a terribly empty feeling ... in your skull?'

'DON'T YOU LOVE NATURE, DESPITE WHAT IT DID TO YOU?'

'Don't you need a licence to be that ugly?'

'Every girl has the right to be ugly, but you abuse the privilege.'

'Go ahead, tell them everything you know. It'll only take ten seconds.'

To which the insulted woman replied:

'I'll tell them everything we both know – it won't take any longer.'

'Have you considered suing your brains for non-support?'

'He has a mind like a steel trap – always closed!'

'HE IS LIVING PROOF THAT MAN CAN LIVE WITHOUT A BRAIN.'

'He is the kind of a man that you would use as a blueprint to build an idiot.'

'He's not stupid; he's just possessed by a retarded ghost.'

'Here's ten pence. Call all your friends and bring back some change.'

'Hi! I'm a human being! What are you?'

'How did you get here? Did someone leave your cage open?'

'I'd like to see things from your point of view but I can't seem to get my head that far up my arse.'

'I bet your brain feels as good as new, seeing that you've never used it.'

'I bet your mother has a loud bark.'

'I could make a monkey out of you, but why should I take all the credit?'

'I don't consider you a vulture. I consider you something a vulture would eat.'

'I don't know what makes you so stupid – but it really works!'

'I don't think you are a fool. But then what's MY opinion against thousands of others?'

'I hear the only place you're ever invited is outside.'

'I hear you were born on a farm. Any more in the litter?'

'I heard you got a brain transplant and the brain rejected you.'

'I HEARD YOU WENT TO HAVE YOUR HEAD EXAMINED BUT THE DOCTORS FOUND NOTHING THERE.'

'I know you are nobody's fool but maybe someone will adopt you.'

'I thought of you all day today ... I was at the zoo.'

'I would ask you how old you are but I know you can't count that high.'

'I'd like to help you out. Which way did you come in?'

'I'd like to leave you with one thought ... but I'm not sure you have a place to put it!'

'I'd love to go out with you, but my favourite commercial is on TV.'

'I'll never forget the first time we met – although I'll keep trying.'

'I'M BUSY NOW. CAN I IGNORE YOU SOME OTHER TIME?'

'I've seen people like you, but I had to pay admission!'

'LOOK AT HIM, LIVING PROOF THAT CARE IN THE COMMUNITY DOESN'T WORK.'

'If I had a face like yours, I'd sue my parents.'

'*If I want any shit out of you I'll squeeze your head.*'

'If ignorance is bliss, you must be the happiest person alive.'

'If we were to kill everybody who hates you, it wouldn't be murder; it would be genocide.'

'If what you don't know can't hurt you, she's invulnerable.'

'*If your brain was chocolate it wouldn't fill an after-eight mint.*'

'Keep talking, someday you'll say something intelligent.'

'*Learn from your parents' mistakes – use birth control.*'

'Look, don't go to a mind reader; go to a palmist. I know you've got a palm.'

'Never enter a battle of wits unarmed.'

'HE'S SO UGLY, MUGGERS GIVE HIM THEIR MASKS TO WEAR.'

'So, a thought crossed your mind? Must have been a long and lonely journey.'

'Some day you will find yourself – and wish you hadn't.'

'Unfortunately, there is no vaccine against stupidity.'

'Whatever is eating you – must be suffering horribly.'

'When you fell out of the ugly tree, you hit every branch on the way down.'

'WHEN YOU WERE A CHILD YOUR MOTHER WANTED TO HIRE SOMEONE TO TAKE CARE OF YOU BUT THE MAFIA WANTED TOO MUCH.'

'You're nobody's fool. Let's see if we can get someone to adopt you.'

'You're so stupid you couldn't pour piss out of a boot if the instructions were on the bottom of the heel.'

'JUST REMEMBER: IF AT FIRST YOU DON'T SUCCEED, BUY HER ANOTHER BEER.'

'Nice shirt. How many cartons of Pot Noodle did you have to eat to get it?'

'Don't look out of the window - people will think that it's Hallowe'en.'

MOTHER IN LAW

'You've a face like a million dollars – all green and wrinkled.'

'At the beautician do you use the emergency entrance?'

'If I ever need a brain transplant, I'd choose yours because I'd want a brain that had never been used.'

'You're a real Action Man: crew cut, realistic scar, and no genitals.'

'Now do you see what happens when cousins marry?'

'I can hardly contain my indifference.'

'When they made you they broke the mould but some of it grew back.'

'Did the aliens forget to remove your probes?'

'Are they your eyeballs? I found them in my cleavage.'

'How many times do I have to flush before you go away?'

'I never forget a face and I can remember both of yours.'

'JUST SMILE AND SAY, "YES MASTER." '

'Mummy, I want to grow up to be neurotic like you.'

'You look like shit, is that the style now?'

'THAT'S A FUN OUTFIT – IT'S FANCY DRESS I PRESUME?'

'NICE DRESS. ARE YOU HOPING TO SLIM INTO IT?'

'He is so ugly they printed his face on airline sick bags.'

'I used to be schizophrenic, but we're OK now.'

'Of course I don't look busy – I did it right the first time.'

'He's multi-talented. He can talk and annoy you at the same time.'

'How can I miss you if you won't go away?'

'You're one of those bad things that happen to good people.'

'If we are what we eat, you're fast, cheap and easy.'

'Sorry if I looked interested – I'm not.'

'I'm not your type – I have a pulse.'

'Yes, it looks like a willy, only smaller.'

'Please keep talking – I need the sleep.'

'I can see your point, but I still think you're full of it.'

'You see ... you should never drink on an empty head.'

'THERE'S NOTHING WRONG WITH YOU THAT REINCARNATION WOULDN'T CURE.'

'I MAY NOT BE THE BEST LOOKING MAN IN HERE BUT I'M THE ONLY ONE TALKING TO YOU.'

'Is that your face or are you trying it out for an ugly sister?'

'Nice hair. Was it that shape when you bought it?'

'I just don't hate myself enough to go out with you.'

'He's not paranoid. Everyone does hate him.'

'Go on, I know you like me – I can see your tail wagging.'

'Her face bears the imprint of the last man who sat on it.'

'I'VE HAD A LOT TO DRINK - YOU'RE BEGINNING TO LOOK HUMAN.'

'Your point has been received, understood and ignored.'

'WERE YOUR PARENTS DISAPPOINTED?'

'You were born a blonde, right?'

'If I need a worthless opinion, I'll ask.'

'If I said you had a beautiful body would you sue me for slander?'

'I bet you wish you'd married her sister / his brother now don't you?'

'Ladies and Gentlemen, tonight we have a member of the local freak show in to give us a solo spot.'

'With a face like that, who needs enemies?'

'YOU MEAN TO SAY THAT WORZEL GUMMIDGE HAD OFFSPRING?'

And:

'I've kept my youthful complexion.'
'Yes, so I see, all spotty.'

'Do you think that I'll lose my looks when I get older?'
'With luck, yes.'

'MY HUSBAND ALWAYS CARRIES MY PHOTO IN HIS
POCKET. IT ONCE SAVED HIS LIVE WHEN A MUGGER
TRIED TO STAB HIM.'
'OF COURSE, YOUR FACE WOULD STOP ANYTHING.'

'I've just come back from the beauty parlour.'
'What a pity it was closed.'

And to finish, a little thought:

It's easy enough to be pleasant,
When life goes along like a song
But the man who's worthwhile
Is the man who can smile
When every bloody thing goes wrong.

(Adolf Hitler 1945)

- Do you speak to your wife while your making love
  - only if she rings
- Does your wife scream while your making love
  - only when she walks in the bedroom
- Her mouth was so big she could sing 2 duets
- I started with nothing and have still got most of it left
- I started at the bottom and sank
- Man with sign - I'm drowning
- My wife has looks that turn stomachs
- Turkey. Your father would turn in his gravy
-